The Cub and His Alphas

Alpha and Omega series #7

By Lisa Oliver

The Cub and His Alphas (Alpha and Omega series #7)

The following trademarks and place names have been used in this work of fiction:

Prius car

The Roswell Alien Museum

Harley Davidson

Facebook

Twitter

Table of Contents

Dedication

There's an awful lot of me and the issues I've been going through in this story, so a huge thank you to all the readers who indulge me by reading it ☺

And no, unfortunately, I am not coming out as a bear shifter… sigh ☺

Author's Note

During the course of this story, my dear bear cub Daniel goes with his mates to a writer's conference in Roswell of all places lol. To give some color to the story, and because my friends have been so helpful to me, I introduced Stormy Glenn and Pat Fischer, who writes as Dani Gray as secondary characters in this story. These two wonderful women are amazing authors in their own right, and them giving me permission to use their names, in my book was the highlight of my day.

To see more of Stormy and Dani's books – please click the links below.

Stormy Glenn on Bookstrand - https://www.bookstrand.com/stormy-glenn

Dani Gray on Bookstrand - https://www.bookstrand.com/dani-gray

Their books are also available on Amazon.

Thank you my friends.

Chapter One

Daniel chuffed as he rubbed his furry back in the long grass, his face turned up to the afternoon sun. Berry bushes, berry bushes as far as the eye could see. Well, they were all Daniel could see, given he was splat dang in the middle of them. *Heaven, heaven, heaven,* he sung in his mind, reaching out with his long claws to snag the nearest branch. *How fucking lucky am I,* he wondered as he smashed a paw-load of blueberries in his mouth.

The run was a spontaneous thing. Daniel was, as a rule, a quiet young man who spent most of his days on the computer writing his latest novel. But today the lure of the sunshine, and a nagging feeling his latest book wasn't going the way it was meant to, saw him taking the four mile drive to his local forest for a bit of a stretch. He had planned on fishing in his furry form, but his nose caught the whiff of ripened fruit and suddenly fish didn't seem as appetizing to his long bear nose.

La, la, la. Daniel swiped more blueberries with his other paw, well aware his golden fur was being stained blue. *Two paw lots, yeah. One lot in my mouth, two lots in my mouth and so much more for me to munch.* He could feel the juices smushed under his nose and dribbling down his chin, but with the sound of the babbling creek he'd planned to fish tickling his ear, Daniel didn't care. He could wash up before he trundled home. The birds were singing, the sun was hot on his fur and the berries were sweet.

Hang on a minute. Daniel tensed and twitched his ears. The birds had been singing, but they were silent now. Seconds later he heard the snap of a breaking twig and the thump of footsteps from a being far heavier than him reverberated up his spine.

Fuck, fuck, fuck, I should have known it was too good to be true. Daniel rolled onto his feet, his fur quivering. Blueberries did grow wild in his part of the world, but what were the chances the perfectly spaced bushes occurred naturally? He was poaching in someone else's patch and as the thuds got closer, Daniel panicked. He didn't know of any other bear shifters in the tiny town of Edendale, but that didn't mean there weren't any. He barely went out.

The bushes to his right rustled and Daniel didn't stick around to find out who he'd pissed off. In bear terms, he was still a cub, only twenty three, and whoever was coming was bigger than him – which took some doing but was possible. *Never get between a bear and his food.* Why his mother's sage piece of wisdom chose to flow through his mind now, Daniel didn't stop to find out. Pushing through the bushes to his left, Daniel put on a burst of speed, running blindly back to where he'd left his car.

Hearing a growl behind him, Daniel risked a quick look over his shoulder. *Two of them, double fuck.* Daniel didn't fight – ever. He liked to joke he was a lover not a fighter, but he was lacking lover experience as well. And if those two lumbering brutes behind him caught up with him, he'd never get a chance to make his dreams a reality.

Got to get to the car, got to get too... shit. Bursting through the tree line, Daniel could have slapped himself for his stupidity, except his paws were too busy trying to put more distance between himself and the bears chasing him. His brand new bright red Prius sat mocking him on the side of the road. Running towards it, Daniel risked another look back. The massive black bears were just coming through the last of the trees. *I don't have time to fucking shift.*

With a lingering whimper as he ran around his car, Daniel took off down the road. His chest was heaving, and the pavement was scorching his paw pads, but Daniel couldn't afford to stop. He'd come back for his car, his phone, his keys, his wallet and everything else he'd left in his 'too-small-for-his-bear-form' vehicle later – a lot later when hopefully the bears chasing him would be gone. *I knew I should have bought a truck.* It was going to be a long run home.

/~/~/~/~/

Zeke raised himself up on his back legs and roared, thumping the roof of the sparkling car with his paw.

"We're going to have to pay to get that repaired," Ty said drily, shaking out his long hair that always seemed to get tangled during a shift. "I hardly think damaging his car is going to endear us to our mate."

Eyeing the sizeable dent in the Prius roof, Zeke thought about tapping beside it to see if he could get it to pop out, but with the size of his paws, it would probably do more damage.

Pulling his raging bear under control he managed a shift, still panting from the run the cub had forced on him. "Why the fuck did he run from us? Is his nose faulty?" Zeke rested his hands on his knees. *Fuck that little cutie can run.*

"It might have had something to do with the fact we were down wind from him, or maybe his nose was full of berry juice. I'm sure the blue on his paws and snout wasn't natural." Ty's voice was calm and logical, just as it always was, although Zeke knew his mate was just as affected by the cub's fear of them as he was. "Either way, we can't hang around out here with our bits dangling. Someone could drive by any minute. I've got the plate number. We'll see if we can hunt him down online when we get back to the motel."

"We were leaving town tomorrow." Zeke straightened, taking a last look down the road before following Ty back into the trees. "Bikes, Blues, and BBQs is on next weekend. You had your heart set on going again this year."

"So, did you," Ty said fondly, taking Zeke's arm as they picked their way across the pine needle strewn ground. The pine needles weren't noticeable against the toughened pads on their paws, but Zeke was looking forward to getting back to where they'd stashed their clothes, so he could put his boots on. His human feet weren't as tough as his bear paws. "I suppose we could still go – give our third a bit of breathing room. Come back after the festival...."

"Now, I know you're teasing." Reaching up, Zeke ruffled Ty's hair before dropping his arm on his mate's shoulders. "There's no way we're going to be happy until that cutie is snuggled up between us, saturated with our spunk."

"You're still as romantic as the day we met." Ty grinned. "But what are the odds, Z? We weren't even going to stop in this blink and you miss it town, although I'm freaking glad we did now."

"The Fates are finally on our side," Zeke agreed. Their decision to stop was based purely on the cute white picket fence the local B and B had as they'd ridden through town. They'd been on the road for days and Ty said he wanted someplace quiet to stay for three or four days before the event the following week.

When they'd mentioned to the sweet Mrs. Cunningham who owned the B&B that they were fond of hiking, she explained anyone could have the run of the forest land provided they didn't light any fires. The opportunity to spend time in their furry form for more than an hour was too good to pass up and for the past three days he and Ty had taken the picnic lunch Mrs. Cunningham provided and headed for the trees.

Reaching the hollowed out tree trunk where they'd stashed their clothes,

Zeke kept out a watchful eye for hikers as Ty poured himself into his jeans. After ten years together, Zeke could still feel a sensual rush through his body as the worn denim molded Ty's thighs and ass perfectly. "You've got that look in your eye again," Ty teased as he pulled his tight muscle shirt over his head and smoothed it over his lean torso. "The one that says you want to drop to your knees and swallow my cock."

"You'd think after all these years you'd know my looks better than that," Zeke grunted. Now Ty was dressed, he could pull on his own clothes. There'd been an incident with some homophobic hunters, in a forest much like the one they were in now, not long after they'd met. Now Zeke always kept his hands free until his mate was fully dressed. "The look I was giving you was I want to bend you over the nearest tree trunk and fuck your ass while you frighten the birds by screaming my name."

"You did that this morning." Ty smirked and then he sighed as he looked back into the forest. "Do you think our cute grizzly is keen on nature sports like the ones we enjoy?"

"It's hard to say." Zeke winced as he stuffed his half-hard cock into his jeans and careful pulled up the zipper. "We haven't noticed the recent scent of any bears since we've been here, and we've covered miles of forest."

"Until today." Ty nodded. "You don't think," he chewed his bottom lip, "you don't think the guy was a tourist, do you? Just passing through?"

Pulling his shirt over his head, Zeke waited until his head was free of the material and then said, "I don't think so. There were no bags or anything in the car that I could see, and besides he wouldn't have left his car if he was traveling. I got the impression he knew where he was going when he took off down the road."

Ty's expression brightened. "Maybe Mrs. Cunningham knows who he is and then we don't have to be racking up favors with your friends in law enforcement, trying to track him on our own. This is a small town and you know what they say about places like this."

"That five minutes after you cough, someone at the other end of town is told you're dying of pneumonia." Zeke laughed. "I'm not sure that'll work in our favor, but we can ask. Or," he picked up their back pack and found their bike keys, "we could just stake out the car until he comes back."

Ty ran his fingers through his hair and then scratched at the four day growth on his chin. "I think I want to freshen up first. We didn't make the best first impression."

"I love it when you're all overgrown and hairy," Zeke growled, dropping the back pack and pulling Ty against his chest. Running his nose along his mate's scruffy jaw, he inhaled sharply. Originally from Alaska, Ty's scent carried a hint of fresh falling snow and a strong undertone of pine. Clean and minty, Zeke always used to think and today was no different. "I don't blame you for wanting to look your awesome best," he whispered against his mate's skin. "But don't forget, he has to take us the way we are, or a mating between us will never work."

"I'm not disputing that, but it won't hurt you to trim up a bit either." Zeke felt a tug on his beard. "That young cub already has to contend with two old Kodiaks as mates. We don't have to give him the impression we're hillbillies as well."

"I prefer the term nomads," Zeke said, rubbing his nose against his mate's. A deep feeling of contentment welled up inside of him. "Maybe now, you'll finally get your wish and we'll have a home to call our own."

"We've had a long run finding our third, Z. Tell me you won't be sorry to give up lumpy mattresses and questionable shower spaces." Ty's hands were warm and familiar on his back and Zeke's body reacted accordingly... and yet, there was something holding him back too and he knew instinctively Ty felt the same way.

"We have to get him to accept us first," Zeke growled. "I'll trim my freaking beard."

"Turn on the charm, big guy. I know you can do it. You snagged me, didn't you?" The twinkle in Ty's eyes were a promise Zeke would cash in on later – when they'd tracked down their runaway cub.

Chapter Two

Three hours later, Daniel was still shivering, in his human form this time. The run home didn't take long, although he had to duck into the trees every time he heard a vehicle coming down the road and he was exhausted by the time he climbed his porch and shifted. One of the things he loved about his home was it was set back a long way from the road, but for the first time ever Daniel wished he lived in the suburbs, or in the middle of town. The sound of other people going about their daily business would be easier to cope with than the oppressive silence around his house.

His shower was a quick affair – the whole time he was washing himself, Daniel fretted he wouldn't be able to hear footsteps approaching over the sound of running water. Dressed in his warmest pullover and thick sweat pants, he still couldn't get warm. He'd tried to write to take his mind off his scare, and gave that up as soon as he started. Staring at the screen and seeing nothing but giant black bears with huge claws and gnashing teeth did nothing for his story line.

It was just a few blueberries. Daniel whimpered and took a sip of his honey tea. Okay, maybe it was three full paws worth of blueberries and he might not have been as considerate about the leaves and branches as he usually would be, *but they'd grow back again.* Daniel couldn't understand it. He'd been on public land – those bushes were available to any number of hikers who wandered through the forests.

Grumpy bears shouldn't have grown them there in the first place. Daniel decided being scared wasn't fun at all. His parents had been academics and he had a quiet and uneventful childhood. The first time he realized the world was a shitty place came when he was fifteen and his parents were killed in a car accident. When the state failed to find any of his relatives, the next three years in state care hadn't been fun, but he learned quickly if he kept his head down and his nose buried in a book most people ignored him. At eighteen Daniel claimed his inheritance and bought his house. Writing, something he'd dabbled with in care, became his full time occupation and as he kept to himself, the opportunities for being scared, *or having a life,* were limited.

"Yeah, well if being scared out of my fur is a definition of living, I'll pass, thank you very much," Daniel said out loud. He glanced at the large railway clock on his wall. It was just after seven. He was going to have to walk back to his car, which on two feet was going to take almost an hour.

It was tempting to leave his brightly colored Prius where it was until morning. The crime rate in Edendale was virtually nonexistent, but if out of town hikers were in the area, then he might find his car a shell of its former self, leaving it out overnight. Besides, his phone was in the car and while it was unlikely anyone was trying to contact him, some of his readers might have tried to message him.

The sum total of my social life, Daniel thought glumly as he washed out his cup and left it to drain before going through to his mudroom and finding his jacket. The days were warm in the autumn, but the nights could get chilly. Shrugging his jacket over his shoulders, Daniel was just about to open his back door, when he heard a rumble that had no business being near his house. "Motorbikes?" They were heading in his direction. "What the fuck?"

Running back through the kitchen, Daniel sprinted upstairs, trying to move as quietly as possible. The upstairs part of his house was split into two huge bedrooms with a bathroom between them. Edging past his huge bed, Daniel flattened himself with his back against the wall, peering around the window frame. The sound of the bikes got louder, ripping apart the silence that usually surrounded Daniel's home, yet when he looked out, he was relieved to see there were only two of them.

Two bears chase me, two bikes come up my driveway, what are the odds this is a coincidence? Zero chance. Daniel weighed up his options. Hiding was his first thought, but his nearest neighbor was five miles towards town and wouldn't hear a thing if his visitors decided to trash his house.

It would be helpful if I had a gun, he thought as the bike engine noise suddenly stopped. But Daniel didn't believe in hunting and never had a need to defend himself or his property. He was larger in his furry form than any of the predators that happened across his back door as a rule. *I'd probably shoot my foot off with the damn thing, anyway.*

No. There was nothing for it. Daniel was going to have to go downstairs and face the intruders. If they weren't related to the bear incident then they'd be human, and Daniel would shift to get rid of them if he had to. Who knows, maybe they were just two lost travelers looking for directions, although Daniel knew that was unlikely. His house couldn't be seen from the road and his driveway could only be found if you knew what to look for.

And if they be bears? Stepping away from the window, Daniel headed back to the stairs, zipping up his fleecy jacket. Maybe the thick layers would prevent him from being slashed too badly. *Who am I kidding. Two big bears could make mincemeat out of me.* Daniel had just got to the bottom of the stairs, when he heard a sharp knocking on his front door. *It was just a few berries, damn it. I do hope these guys will be reasonable.*

His hand trembled as he reached for the door handle.

/~/~/~/~/

"Wow, this is amazing. Are you sure we've got the right place?" Ty asked as he turned off his bike and sat for a moment appreciating the scenery and serenity that scenery offered. The house was more of a log cabin, although Ty noted the second story extension and the new aluminum joinery that housed huge picture windows right around the house. All he could see for miles around was lush grasslands and pockets of bush. The house sat at the base of a tall gently sloping hill topped with huge slabs of rock. Ty could imagine how they'd look in winter, all covered in snow. A chimney perched on the roof suggested warm fires and somewhere to snuggle on a cold night.

"Mrs. Cunningham said twelve miles from town, look for the big willow and turn left there. This is it." Zeke gave a low whistle as he looked around. "I know the land is cheap around here, but this had to have cost some money. Do you think our cub comes from a rich family?"

"Mrs. C said this Daniel barely has any visitors, and is always quiet and politely spoken when he goes to town. She never mentioned him being flashy with money." Ty shrugged. "I guess we'll find out in due course. Are you ready for this?" Ty definitely was. Even now, sitting outside the house, his bear was alert, urging him closer to the huge double front doors.

"What if he has got something wrong with his sense of smell and doesn't realize who we are to him? Or maybe he was raised with humans and doesn't know about the concept of mates. What do we do then?" Zeke swung his leg over his bike and straightened the button down shirt Ty encouraged him to wear.

"Then we talk to him." Ty chuckled as he got off his bike. "I know it's not your strongest skill, big guy, but you can do it." Stepping closer to his mate, he whispered quietly, "I've waited eighty odd years for this day to come; I know for you it's been over a hundred. We gave up our lives, our homes and everything else, to follow the path the fates set for us, just so we could find our third. In the ten years we've been together, I've never doubted that decision or my feelings for you. Whatever or whoever is behind that door, we'll handle it, just like we always have – together."

"Are you going to get all mushy on me?" Zeke scowled, and Ty's grin got wider. He could tell by his mate's eyes Zeke was just as excited as he was.

"It wouldn't hurt for you to dust off a few mushy skills of your own. Not everyone is as blown away with your rustic charm as I am. Now come on." Ty flicked his head towards the door. "The cub must have heard us coming. It's time for us to introduce ourselves, and for goodness sake, break out that smile of yours." He showed his teeth.

"Shave my head, trim my beard, wear a shirt and now he wants me to smile," Zeke muttered, but he did relax his face from its customary snarl.

Bounding up the few steps to the porch, Ty strode across the planks and rapped smartly at the door. For the first time since that heady night when he met Zeke, his stomach was a flutter of excitement. The trace of jasmine and bear lingered around the door, causing his cock to firm up. His keen ears picked up the sound of footsteps and after a long moment, the door opened.

Ty's mouth dropped open.

/~/~/~/~/

Please don't let there be drool in my whiskers. A log cabin in a remote area housing a bear shifter, Zeke imagined their third as someone with a black bushy beard, red flannelette shirts, maybe a bit of softness around his middle, carrying an ax over his shoulder. The vision framed by the door couldn't be further from that image. *Fucking hell, what on earth did we do to deserve such perfection?*

Their cub, and the scent coming from the young man definitely confirmed that aspect, was about a foot shorter than Zeke's six foot six. His pale face was highlighted by two patches of pink on his high cheeks and framed by untidy shoulder length blond hair. But it was their third's lips that captured Zeke's attention. Full, wide and pink. Zeke swallowed a groan as he imagined what those lips could do with a spot of encouragement.

"Can I help you?" Daniel stepped closer and Zeke was hit with the full force of his third's scent. The delicious smell made him want to rip that ridiculously bulky jacket from his mate's body and strip him bare, maybe slathering him with honey so he and Ty could have a feast. Ty. Why wasn't Ty saying anything? He was the smooth talker in their partnership. A quick glance to his side showed Ty was as dumbstruck as he was.

"Er, hello." Zeke decided to take the initiative and stuck out his hand. "I'm Zeke McIntyre and this is my partner Ty Hollifield. We've come to apologize. We think we might have frightened you in the forest this afternoon."

"Daniel Borden." Daniel's hand slipped into his and electricity sparked its way up Zeke's arm, causing all his body hair to stand up on end. He couldn't let go. There wasn't a force on earth that would make him let go of Daniel's hand. Instead, Zeke pulled his mate close and buried his nose against the wee strip of skin poking above Daniel's coat collar. A rumbling groan forced its way out of his chest and throat.

"Zeke!"

There was a hint of worry in Ty's tone. Enough for Zeke to raise his head long enough to say, "Fuck, you've got to smell him. You've got to scent our Daniel."

"I can, I did, I do," Ty said, and Zeke noticed he was standing behind their third. "But don't you think he should be conscious before we do anything else?"

Conscious? Zeke looked down. Daniel's head was lolling to one side, his neck arched, his lips slack. The reason he was upright was because of Ty's arms holding him up. "Oops. What do you think happened?"

"From the way his heart started racing and the scent of his arousal increased, I'd like to think our mate came to the same conclusion we did. However, it's a little hard to tell now. He could have just been overcome by a huge bald man who wanted to rub his beard on his neck."

"Well, shit." Zeke patted the hand he was still holding. Then the side of his lip quirked up. "As his mates its only right and proper we should get young Daniel inside – make sure he's warm and comfortable. It's not as though we can leave him alone, defenseless at night, when he's unconscious."

"And once we're in, we can work on the charm aspect." Ty winked. "Grab his feet, big guy. I could carry him myself, but I figure you don't want to let go of him either."

You've got that right. Resting Daniel's hand on his chest, Zeke bent and scooped his arm behind Daniel's knees. The young man would be lucky if he weighed a buck twenty and most of that was probably jacket. Zeke was determined to shred that at the first possible opportunity. His mate would need leathers to ride on the back of the bikes, and when he wasn't riding, Zeke and Ty would keep him warm. *I must have been a very, very good boy in a past life,* he thought as he and Ty carried Daniel inside.

Chapter Three

Daniel stirred, immediately aware he was lying on his couch, still dressed although his jacket was missing. *I don't remember lighting a fire,* he thought as he heard the crackle of wood, and picked up the faint scent of smoke. And then the events of the evening came flooding back to him and he slapped a hand over his mouth to hold back his gasp. There were two men, *his freaking mates* and they actually knocked on his fucking door – something all romance novels claimed never happened, but it did. It happened to him.

But where were the two hunks now? Daniel was stunned he'd been so blessed in the mate department. So, blessed he'd actually swooned when the one called Zeke sniffed at him. He couldn't help himself – the overwhelming scent, the fact there was two of them… not a good way to make a solid first impression.

Daniel's father mentioned, when they had "that talk" when he was twelve, that it was possible, if he found a fated mate, that he'd end up with two of them. Apparently, it was important among bears to mention that to a significant other, if the person was single when they met. A distant relative of his father's had found one mate, and then been accused of cheating when he bumped into the second one in the grocery store. It wasn't until the first mate scented the second that all was forgiven. So, having two mates wasn't a shock. The fact they ticked every single one of his fantasy boxes was. Daniel couldn't even dream up men as sexy as the ones he'd met.

The one who introduced himself as Zeke – *walking biker bad boy fantasy* – fascinated Daniel because he shaved his head. Most shifters liked to keep their hair long. And he had hair on his arms – almost unheard of for a shifter. Daniel wondered if he had hair anywhere else. And Ty; oh, my gods, Ty was just as tall and slightly more streamlined, but he looked like he'd walked off the page of a magazine. Daniel's whole body trembled with the idea of getting to know them both.

Keeping his eyes closed, Daniel used his other senses to see where the men had gone. Their scent was fresh, so they hadn't left. Not that Daniel expected them to. He'd been hunted down, and Daniel sent a small prayer of thanks to whoever told them where he lived. It wasn't as though his house was on the main road. Ah, they were in the kitchen. Daniel's lips twitched as he listened to the two men banter. He guessed they'd been together for a while.

"How many boxes of tea does one person need?" That gravelly voice had to be Zeke. "He's got at least eight different types, plus three brands of coffee, and chocolate."

"We need to find the one he uses the most." Ty's sultry tones made

Daniel's toes curl. "It's important we show him we can take care of all his needs from the start."

"It would help if he didn't have such a huge collection of beverages." Zeke grumbled. "Look at this. Jasmine, blackberry, Earl Gray, lemon, lemon and honey, lemon and ginger, chamomile. None of that sounds comforting to me."

"They probably all are in their own way, big guy. Coffee would be stimulating, but after a shock, Daniel won't need that. What about hot chocolate?"

"Do you know how to work his machine? I sure as hell don't." Zeke sounded peeved as though Daniel's state of the art coffee machine insulted him.

"I could make it the old fashioned way. Heat the milk on the stove." Daniel heard the sound of cupboard doors opening. "See if you can find marshmallows."

More opening and closing cupboard doors and the sound of a pan going on the hot plate. Then there was a hushed whisper from Zeke. "Do you think he has a favorite mug?"

"We don't want to come off as stalkers," Ty admonished. "Just get three mugs from the mug tree. I'm sure he won't mind."

"Oh my god, he's got peanut snicker bars." Daniel stifled a groan. Zeke had found his stash. "Do you know how yummy these are? He has a whole box full of them." Daniel could hear the rustle of paper and some heavy duty chomping going on.

"Zeke!" Ty hissed. "Don't stuff half a dozen of them in your mouth at once. We're trying to make a good impression."

"So am I." Zeke's words were muffled. "I'm showing my mouth is big enough to suck you both off at the same time. He'll appreciate that."

The mental imagery was too much for Daniel. He shoved his hand down his pants to pull the material away from his growing dick. Ty's answering laugh didn't help. Every time he opened his mouth, Daniel wanted to melt. *How the hell am I going to get anything done with two of them around all the time?* But would they be around? That was a sobering thought. Daniel's bear let him know his mates were considerably older than him. They probably already had a home, and businesses or something somewhere else. Hell, they could have ex-wives and a dozen kids for all Daniel knew. And it would just be his luck those kids would probably be older than him.

"Hi there, having fun?" Ty's teasing tone had Daniel's eyes flying open. Ty and Zeke were both standing by the edge of the couch. Following Ty's gaze, Daniel glanced down, and his cheeks flamed as he hastily pulled his hand out of his pants.

"Er... things were getting a bit constricted." Daniel didn't know where to look.

"I know exactly what you mean, cutie." Zeke blatantly adjusted his bulge with one hand, holding out a mug of hot chocolate with the other. "Can we sit down?"

"Of course." Taking the mug Ty offered him, Daniel stared at the swirl of chocolate peppered with three large marshmallows. It smelled amazing. "Thank you."

Of course, the bears would have to sit on either side of him, reminding Daniel of how puny he was in comparison to them. "It was kinda Zeke's fault you fainted anyway," Ty said, winking at the man mentioned. "He can come on a bit strong, but he has a heart of gold underneath all those muscles."

"You're both... er..." Daniel tried to think how he would describe them in a story, "well-blessed in the muscle department. Unlike me," he added.

"You're a beautifully sexy cub." Zeke took a large slurp of his drink and sighed. "What did you need to know about us before we get to the fun part of the evening?"

"Zeke," Ty's shocked tone made Daniel chuckle. "We want to get to know our mate. He's young. Show some patience. I'm sorry, Daniel. You'll get used to Zeke's blunt manner."

"It's fine." Daniel was suddenly shy and took a quick sip of his drink. The marshmallows were melting and one stuck to his top lip and he quickly licked it off, conscious of Zeke's heated gaze burning his cheeks. "So, you, you chased me in the forest because I was your mate? Not because I was eating your blueberries?"

"They weren't ours." Zeke finished off his drink in two large swallows and put the mug on Daniel's coffee table. "They were a good find though, cub. If I hadn't been so hell bent on chasing your ass, I'd have stopped for a feed myself. The only thing smelling sweeter than those berries was you."

"Oh. Thank you." Daniel risked a quick look at Ty who was beaming at his mate. "Are you guys locals? I've got to admit, I don't know many people in town."

To Daniel's disappointment, Ty shook his head. "No. We've been traveling all over the country the past ten years. There's nothing like being on the open road, the wind in your hair, moving from place to place, always meeting new people and sharing new experiences."

"That sounds… nice." Daniel's insides shriveled up and he wanted to curl in on himself. Sitting between two of the sexiest men he'd ever seen was playing havoc with his libido, but somehow, he didn't think his mates were going to stick around and that made Daniel feel sick. "Did you think you might come back and visit sometimes? I mean, not that you have to or anything, but...." *Shit. I should've known this was too good to be true.*

"Hey. What's all this about us visiting?" Zeke growled. "Are you saying you don't want us to live with you when we're mated?"

"No, I mean yes, I mean..." Daniel took a deep breath and let it out slowly. "I was raised to believe mates stayed together, couldn't bear to be apart. But if you're always on the road, traveling around...."

"Oh shit, I'm sorry, Daniel, I should have explained in more detail." Ty put his mug on the table and grabbed Daniel's hand in his. "We've been traveling for the past ten years searching for *you*. We always knew we'd be a triad. When one didn't show up the first year we got together, we decided to come and look for you. Yes, it's been fun, all the traveling and the new experiences, but our goal was to find you, and now we have."

That brightened Daniel's perspective. "If you'd found me ten years ago, you'd have been disappointed," Daniel managed a small grin. "I was only thirteen." Then he thought about his parents' death and spending that time in care and his mood dropped. If his mates had been around, even if they couldn't claim him, it would have been better than living in a foster home, and he could have had more fun on his eighteenth birthday, than spending his day haggling with the family lawyer.

"Hey, why the change in mood, cub?" Zeke's arm was solid on his shoulder. "Didn't you have a good childhood?"

Daniel nodded, tears prickling his eyes. He quickly explained about his parents dying and his search for a home to call his own. "That's why I didn't want to leave here," he whispered, "I know it's kinda silly, but

I thought if I owned my own home, then no more bad things could happen to me. I'd have my own safe place."

"You've got a lovely home," Ty was quick to assure him. Somehow, during Daniel's confession he was now being hugged by both of them, and it felt kinda nice. Sweaty, especially with the fire still going, but nice. "Do you think you've got room in this safe space of yours for two crusty Kodiaks?"

"Ty's been longing to settle down," Zeke explained as Daniel struggled to pull any words out of his mouth. "We both had homes when we met, but they were at opposite ends of the country. Rather than settle in one, we decided to sell up and hit the road. We figured, if our third didn't have a home, then we'd get one together somewhere, but what you have here is perfect."

Swallowing hard, Daniel managed to ask. "Won't you miss all the excitement, and meeting new people, being out on the road and things like that?"

Ty looked at Zeke who shook his head. "We can still go on road trips, take you with us. That is, if you can take time off from whatever it is you do. Do you work someplace close?"

"My office is just down the hall." Daniel tilted his head in that direction. "I work from home. I'm a self-published romance writer." His cheeks heated and that had nothing to do with the warm fire, or sitting between his mates. Two big bikers weren't likely to read the type of romances he churned out.

But Ty looked excited. "MM, MF, MFM, MMM, PNR? I bet you write paranormal, am I right?"

Daniel was surprised. "MM, MMM, and PNR, yep. I write mostly about bear shifters."

"Ooh, I bet I've got some of your books." Using his free hand, Ty pulled out his phone and clicked on his Amazon app.

"Ty reads for a couple of hours every chance he gets," Zeke said fondly. "What name do you write under?"

"D.B. Bear," Daniel mumbled. He didn't think he was a total loser as a writer. He made enough money every month to pay his bills, but it wasn't as though he'd won any awards or anything.

"Oh, my gods, I know that name." Ty stabbed his screen. "You're writing the 'Everlast' series. I've got every one of your books and I've been checking out Amazon every chance I get for the next one. Tell me Xander gets his mate at last, please, pretty please? Is it that cute little hottie from the coffee shop, or someone else?"

"You really do read them." Stunned, Daniel didn't know what to say. He'd never met anyone in person who'd read his books before.

"You know," Zeke growled, leaning heavily on Daniel's shoulders, "you write some pretty hot and heavy sex scenes between those characters of yours. Are you writing from experience?"

"No, I don't and before you ask if I get aroused writing a sex scene, that's got nothing to do you or anyone else." Unable to move out from under Zeke's arm without sitting on Ty's lap, Daniel lurched forward, turning to perch his ass on the coffee table instead. "I'm a normal healthy bear and I have perfectly natural needs. The energies that come from any arousal I feel when writing is poured back into my stories. That's it."

Ty and Zeke exchanged glances. "It seems like we hit on a trigger topic for you, mate. It wasn't intentional," Ty said gently. "Want to explain what all that's about? Have you had bad experiences with assholes in the past?"

Daniel immediately felt silly. He was overreacting and now he was going to have to explain the most humiliating aspect of his life. "I tried dating a few times, once everything was worked out with the lawyer and before I bought this place. My first ever book was getting some decent reviews online and I thought I could do anything. I was young, single, and for the first time, I was free to date."

"What happened?" Zeke growled, leaning forward and resting his elbows on his knees. Daniel noticed Ty was sitting the same way. *A sexy set of bookends,* he thought, but decided his urge to laugh wasn't appropriate.

"Did someone hurt you?" Where Zeke bristled with protectiveness, Ty just seemed concerned.

"It never got to that stage," Daniel admitted quietly, staring down at his hands. "I signed up on a few sites and got a fair bit of interest. Most of them were jerks sending out dick pictures, just out for a fuck, but a couple of men seemed nice, so I started chatting with them. They'd ask what I do, and then when I told them, the jokes would start about me masturbating at my desk, and asking me how many keyboards I went through because they'd get covered in spunk every day. They all thought I just wrote porn. Then there were the guys who wanted to know if we could act out the scenes I wrote, or who offered to help me research kinkier sex scenes. It was like no one could see past what I did for a living. In the end I gave up looking and deleted my profiles."

He'd been honest. His mates could read between the lines. Despite his house and his career, Daniel knew he was a loser in all other aspects of life. Shit, he didn't even have any real life friends. Well, now his mates knew it too. He wondered if they'd even kiss him before they made their excuses and left.

Chapter Four

Ty's heart melted as he took in the slumped shoulders and downcast look of their new mate. Daniel confirmed what he'd already suspected – he was very young, and while adult in human years at twenty three – in shifter terms he was still a cub. A lonely, beautiful cub. The dispassionate way Daniel described being in care; Ty couldn't believe a shifter still coming to terms with his shift was then thrust into a human foster care system and expected to cope with the added hassles of keeping his animal side hidden. But Daniel did cope and came out stronger because of it.

He hadn't been lying when Ty said he remembered Daniel's books. Daniel was a one-click auto buy for him and he and Zeke had spent many a sexy night in a random hotel or motel room, Ty reading out loud the next installment. *To think, all this time, we've been learning about our mate with every scintillating page.* Every story was filled with action and a ton of heat, showing a depth of maturity and an understanding of relationships, suggesting an author a lot older.

And yet their mate was a virgin – a sweet, untried, and now horrifically embarrassed virgin. Glancing over at Zeke, Ty saw his concern mirrored in his mate's green eyes. Zeke wouldn't want to say anything, because comforting wasn't his strongest skill and he'd worry anything he said would make the situation worse. Inhaling softly, Ty reached over and took Daniel's hand. "I can't believe what a treasure you are," he said, keeping his voice low. "You forged a successful life for yourself, created a beautiful home and a solid career and you did it all with no guidance from anyone. You have so much to be proud of."

Daniel looked up, a furrow between his eyes. "I have the social skills of a lump of wood. The only people I really chat to are online friends who read my stories. I venture into town once a month to buy supplies and can barely think to respond to questions about the weather. You two… you… you…."

"I've been around for over a century," Zeke rumbled. "Ty will tell you – when we met my idea of being social was refraining from hitting someone in the face when they said something as banal as 'nice weather we're having for this time of year,'."

"It's true," Ty chuckled, rubbing his thumb over Daniel's pulse point. "I was working nights in a fancy gay club when we met and Zeke bursts in all macho in his leathers and his hairy chest. As you can imagine, half the wee twinks in the place all wanted to fall to their knees and worship his cock, but he didn't pay them any mind at all, just shoving them out of the way when they got in front of him."

"My bear scented you. I didn't see anyone else."

"Wow, that's like a scene from a love story," Daniel's eyes were wide. "What happened then?"

"Well, if it'd been one of your romances we would have met in the center of the room, he would have swept me into his arms and we'd seal our deal with a kiss, with all the wee twinks dabbing their eyes with their tissues." Ty shook his head. "It didn't quite happen like that."

"That guy shouldn't have tripped you." Zeke took Daniel's other hand. "My bear was on a mission. I could barely hold him back from shifting. I could sense it, the second Ty realized who I was to him, and thankfully he moved in my direction."

"You can picture the scene," Ty laughed, remembering it as though it was yesterday. "Glitzy club complete with disco ball, loud music, plenty of flesh showing and everyone drinking those damn cocktails with umbrellas in them. Somehow, in all the chaos it was as though my bear sensed Zeke as soon as he came through the door. I was carrying this tray of drinks and I twisted to put it on a table, and this guy came out of nowhere and tripped me up tray and all, and I fell on a heap of broken glass and booze."

"He deliberately stuck out his foot," Zeke scowled. "He was lucky he escaped with a black eye and a broken nose."

"And the two bouncers were just doing their jobs when they tried to kick you out? One of them ended up with a broken jaw," Ty laughed.

"Really?" Daniel's eyes were like saucers. "What happened? Did you get into trouble?"

"This one convinced me to run with him." Zeke shook his head although the edges of his lips were turned up. "I could've taken them all, but no, Ty decided he didn't want his mate beat up, and dragged me out of there before the police were called."

"That didn't stop that little guy, what was his name? Anyhow, not important, but yeah, this little twink with more balls than most, came running after us, begging to come with us." Ty burst out laughing. "I thought you were going to shift then and there, rip out his balls and shove them down his throat."

"Damn idiot knew nothing about mates. He should've known better than to get in our way," Zeke grumbled. "Speaking of tempers though...."

Oh my god, he's going to tell Daniel about his car. Ty stroked up Daniel's arm and waited for the fireworks.

/~/~/~/~/

There wasn't a thing in the world Zeke was scared of – well, except for big hairy spiders, but that was perfectly normal and nothing to be ashamed of – but he knew, after being with Ty for so long mostly, that he really needed to tell Daniel about the damage to his car before they could claim each other, and that worried him. Daniel had that look about him that was all innocence and honey wouldn't melt in his mouth, but after hearing about his time in care, Zeke knew his mate was made of stronger stuff.

He tried smiling. Ty swore it was the best way to make someone feel relaxed. But then, he had a full beard, so maybe his smile wouldn't be noticeable, so he stretched his mouth further and that made his cheeks ache. And it wasn't as though he could talk with a huge cheesy grin on his face. In the meantime, Ty was trying not to laugh, and Daniel was looking between the pair of them, his full bottom lip snagged in his teeth.

"Just tell him, already," Ty nudged him with his elbow. "He'll understand."

"You're not into some kind of pain kink, are you?" Daniel's body was so stiff he was vibrating.

"No, no, nothing like that," Zeke said quickly, giving up on trying to rearrange his face. His words were more important. "Look, sometimes I get frustrated and tend to lash out at things. I would never hurt you or Ty, EVER," he added quickly as Daniel's eyes threatened to fall out. "My bear would never allow me to lash out at you, that's not the way bears are with fated mates. Surely your parents taught you that much at least."

Daniel nodded tightly. Zeke covered the hand he was holding with his other hand. "You ran from us, in the forest. I didn't realize you couldn't scent us. I got a bit frustrated."

"All I could smell was the blueberries," Daniel admitted. "What did you do, knock down a tree?"

"I thumped the roof of your car." Zeke tilted his head slightly and tried that grin again.

"While you were still in fur?" Daniel's voice rose, and he pulled both his hands free. Zeke leaned back as his mate stood up, his hands resting on his slender hips. "You used your bear strength on my pristine BRAND NEW car?"

From where Zeke was sitting, Daniel was looming above him like a slender angel. Unable to help himself, Zeke's eyes roamed his mate's body noting the long legs, heaving chest and prominent bulge in the groin area. This time his smirk came unbidden. Their new mate was gorgeous.

"Don't you dare laugh at me," Daniel fumed. "I saved for over a year to buy that car. I only had it delivered three weeks ago. Now, you're telling me it's got a bear sized dent in the roof? What the hell is the insurance going to say? What am I going to tell them? Oh, don't worry about it, it was just some pissy bear who objected because I ran from him when he was chasing me, like any sane person would do?"

"Actually, wild life guides suggest you should never run from a bear, because they can run faster," Zeke said in what he hoped was a reasonable tone. "Climbing a tree would be safer, if you are fast enough and can climb high enough. Otherwise you're supposed to curl up on your side...."

"Tell that to my Prius," Daniel yelled. "It was just a dumb, inanimate object who happened to get in the way of your thumping great paw. What are you going to do about my dented roof?" He leaned over, his finger pointed aiming for Zeke's chest, but Daniel misjudged the distance. Seconds later, Zeke found himself with an armful of cub and he groaned, his arms coming up instinctively, to hold the younger man close.

"Don't you get fresh with me." Daniel struggled to get out of Zeke's hold, but Zeke wasn't letting go. "I'm still mad about my car. You're not going to sex me out of being angry."

Zeke could see Daniel's mouth was moving, but he couldn't hear the words. The rush of blood throughout his whole body was roaring in his ears, his bear hovering close to the surface. All Zeke could smell was the sweet scent of his mate, infused with the delicious aroma of arousal. Those lips were moving – tempting him with their fullness and Zeke couldn't think – all he could do was act. Catching Daniel's hair in one hand, holding him tight with the other, he pressed his lips against Daniel's and groaned again at the fresh new sensation. *Oh, yummy.* His bear settled as Zeke got onto the serious business of kissing the anger out of his feisty mate. *Hey, it could work.*

Chapter Five

Daniel couldn't think – hell, he could barely breathe. Zeke's lips were like a zap of lightening that lit the slow burn in his belly and turned it into a wildfire. Hundreds of words he'd written about kissing couples – thousands of them – and none of them prepared him for the real life experience.

Zeke's lips were hard and warm; the hairs of his moustache tickled Daniel's nose. The hair under Zeke's chin was as soft as Daniel imagined, rubbing against his face. Zeke's grip in his hair was firm, his blunt nails on Daniel's scalp sending tingles through his whole body. When Zeke finally released his hold, Daniel was gasping for air, aware he'd been angry about something, but he was damned if he could remember what it was. He could barely remember his name.

"Yum, that looked hot. My turn." Ty was there, behind him, and before Daniel had a chance to open his mouth his second kiss of his life was happening and there was nothing Daniel could do about it. Not that he wanted to, because damn, his men seemed to know what they were doing. He flailed his arms as Ty pulled him backwards, finding the rock hard muscles of Zeke's chest with one hand and Ty's broad shoulder with the other.

Mmm, petting. Petting seemed like a good idea and it wasn't as though either man was complaining. Ty was busy trying to find his tonsils with his tongue, and Zeke... well, Daniel wasn't sure what Zeke was doing, but the bulge under his ass seemed to be getting bigger and there were hands all over him, stroking his skin, finding their way under his clothes. His own cock, starved for attention for what felt like forever, threatened to spill in his pants, and in a panic, Daniel pulled his lips free. "Stop, stop, I'm going to come," he panted.

"That was the intention," Zeke growled and then Ty took his mouth again, harder and with more urgency than before. Daniel figured it was Zeke demolishing his zipper, but he really didn't care who it was. When work-roughened hands grasped his shaft, Daniel screamed down Ty's throat as his balls unloaded.

Oh, my, gods, who knew it could feel that good. But even as his body sighed with relief as a flood of feel-good hormones swept through his body, Daniel stiffened with embarrassment and his second 'oh my gods' was for a totally different reason this time. *What the hell must they think of me? I couldn't even last five minutes.*

/∼/∼/∼/∼/

Ty could sense it, the moment Daniel's embarrassment hit. Their sweet mate had responded so beautifully, and if he and Zeke could bring his mate off with a single kiss, then the rest of their bedroom antics were going to be hot. But for now, he reminded himself their sweet Daniel was a virgin. If those weren't his first kisses, it was close and from the way Daniel's cock blew the second he was touched, it was clear Daniel wasn't used to anyone else handling that part of him either.

Which in turn, brought out all of Ty's protective instincts. Tugging his hair away from one side of his neck, he rested Daniel's head, so the cub's nose was full of his scent. "So beautiful, babe. So beautiful." Just having Daniel so close, in his arms with Zeke stroking his lower back was enough to set his balls pulsing with need.

"I think," Ty coughed and tried again. "I'm thinking me and Zeke should probably go and get your car, if that's all right with you. Before it gets much later. I know you're worried, with the dent and all, but I promise it's not too bad, and we may be able to pop it out and clean it up without any insurance company involvement. We could bring it back here for you...."

"That's it?" Daniel raised his head. "You wank me off and throw out a few kisses and then you want to leave? Fine. Whatever." He scrambled off Zeke's lap and out of Ty's arms. "Don't let the door hit you on the way out." He stumbled once, grabbing at his still open pants. Ty reached to help him, but Daniel evaded his grasp, storming upstairs. Seconds later a door slammed.

"Not your smoothest move, sweetness." Zeke grinned ruefully, wiggling his ass in an effort to accommodate the bulge in his pants.

"Well, I need a fucking fuck," Ty hissed, pissed off his efforts at being nice were taken the wrong way. "There's no way our sweet cub is ready to take a pounding from us yet. I thought we could head out, take care of our needs real quick, grab the car and come back." He sighed as he thought of Daniel's reaction. "Shit. I was being selfish, wasn't I? Damn it. It was a dumb thing to say. He probably thinks we aren't coming back. That I was just making excuses for us to get out of here."

"Probably, but I think we should go ahead with your plan anyway," Zeke stretched and got to his feet. "The only way we can prove to him we're reliable is by going and coming back. Besides, you're not the only one all hot and bothered. Did you see our cub's face when he climaxed? I've never seen anything so hot, unless it's your face when your balls erupt."

Ty chuckled. Zeke wasn't known for sweet phrases, or words of love, but that didn't mean he didn't have those feelings. He just didn't express them as easily as Ty did. "Kissing someone without all that facial hair was a novelty. It was good too, wasn't it?"

"Different, but just as good as you."

Aww. Ty knew what Zeke was trying to do. He got up, leaning his head on

Zeke's shoulder. "I'm not going to get upset or jealous if you say something nice about our cub to me, and I don't expect you to get jealous if I do the same thing. We went into our mating, eagerly anticipating meeting our third. I have always loved you and that will never change. But my heart has always had a Daniel-sized hole in it and I'm sure yours does too. My only hope is that Daniel doesn't feel threatened by our ten year history. We've shared a lot of fun and hot times together."

"And they aren't over," Zeke reminded him. "It's just now they'll include all three of us and now we have a home base. If, we get our asses into gear and prove to our cub we can be trusted."

Ty nodded, and they moved towards the door. "I will say this, though." He looked up the stairs where Daniel had disappeared to. "I'm glad he doesn't look like you or me. I'm glad he's got his own uniqueness. I think it would be weird if he looked like either of us."

"It's kinda nice he's smaller than us too," Zeke agreed, holding the door open for Ty. "Brings out my latent protective urges."

"Mine too." Ty raised his voice. "We'll be back soon, cub. Some coffee would be nice and don't let the fire go out."

He tilted his head, but got no reply. "We'd better make that a super quick fuck," he whispered.

"That won't be difficult, babe." Checking to make sure the snib was off the lock, so they could get back in, Zeke closed the door behind them.

/~/~/~/~/~/

They expect me to make coffee? Daniel wasn't sure if he wanted to kick someone or break down and cry as he heard a single bike start up and take off down the driveway. He was only half way up his stairs when it hit him how childish he was being. He was the one who kicked up a fuss about his car. He didn't even try to reciprocate the sexy interlude they offered him, although in his defense he couldn't even think straight at the time. But no, as soon as Ty mentioned going out to collect his car, he stormed off like a two-year old, his pants still open and spunk drying around his junk.

And you know why you stormed off, don't you, Daniel argued with himself as he pulled a fresh pair of jeans from his dresser and went through into the bathroom. *Because you've got two strapping hunky males who took the time to work together to get you off, and you didn't have a clue what to do in return. You're a fucking embarrassment.*

And that was the sad truth of the matter. Daniel scrubbed away the evidence, his cheeks burning as hot as his swollen lips. Every sex scene he'd ever written was based on his dreams and research, and despite getting copious positive reviews for the things he'd written, one kiss from Zeke and Ty let Daniel know how woefully inadequate the internet could be for the research side of things. It was rare to find true MM couples' porn on the sites Daniel frequented, and even the few he did find were usually BDSM couples, which was not something Daniel included in his stories – again, because he didn't believe he knew enough about the scene.

Are you going to let your fears define you? His father's voice whispered through his head. Zipping up his jeans, Daniel leaned against the bathroom counter, blinking rapidly. Eight long years his parents had been gone. For the most part, Daniel had come to terms with their accident, keeping himself busy so he didn't dwell on what might have been. His parents were quiet, like him, and always had their heads buried in books. Yet, the moment he asked to talk to either one of them, they always put down what they were doing and gave him their complete attention.

I miss you both so much, Daniel thought as his heart squeezed painfully. He wasn't sure what his parents would have thought about Zeke and Ty. They seemed to get on with anyone they came in contact with, but like Daniel, they preferred a quiet home life. Daniel thought back to the one time his mom sat him down and talked about true mates. He remembered it as though it was yesterday. The bright checkered table cloth, his mom was making honey muffins and she'd asked Daniel to help her.

"It wouldn't hurt for you to learn how to make these," his mom said, stirring the contents of the bowl briskly. *"The way to any man's heart is through is stomach."*

"How do you know my mate will be a man?" Daniel was fourteen and was

only just coming to terms with the people in his fantasies. His mom smiled and winked, and Daniel put it down to "mom knows best", something his mom was fond of saying. "What's it like having a true mate?"

"It's like finding your very best friend, your hottest lover, and your staunchest protector all in the one person – or in a bear's case, sometimes two of them." His mom handed him the scoop and bowl and Daniel carefully measured out enough batter to half fill the patty tins. "The thing you need to remember about true mates is that they will never lie to you, never cheat on you, and always have your best interests at heart. They might not be perfect – it would be a boring life if they were, but you can guarantee that everything your mate says will be the truth. You will always be able to trust them, no matter what they say or do. That's what makes having a *relationship with mates so wonderful."*

The memory faded from Daniel's mind and he was back, holding onto the bathroom counter, applying his mom's words to his current situation. Ty said they'd be back. Daniel needed to trust that. And he asked for coffee, and he wanted the fire kept going. Daniel could do that too. *One step at a time,* he cautioned himself as he headed back down the stairs. His mates knew he was a virgin. That didn't seem to bother them. He could learn how to please them over time. *Real life research this time.* Daniel gave a quick fist pump as his spirits rose and hurried into the kitchen.

Chapter Six

The lights were off upstairs in Daniel's house when Zeke followed the car, Ty was driving, up the driveway. "Good sign, or bad sign?" Ty asked, unfolding himself from the small car and locking it with a click. He had a phone and wallet in his hand, Zeke assumed they were Daniel's, and a worried look on his flushed face as he looked up at the dark second story.

"It won't make no never mind." Getting off his bike, Zeke pulled a leaf out of Ty's hair. "We're not going anywhere, and if he's locked the door on us, we'll camp on the porch. It won't be the worst place we've slept together."

"The lights are still on downstairs. Oh, Zeke, we've waited so fucking long for this day. What if I've fucked things up already?"

Of the two of them, Ty was the more sensitive and a people person which was the perfect foil for Zeke's gruffer nature. It was typical Ty would take Daniel's storming off to heart. "I was the one who dinged his car," he reminded his mate gently. "You can hide behind me when he yells at me for the damage." It was a very large dent on a very small car.

"We're a pair of nutters, aren't we?" Ty chuckled. "Daniel is our mate. Even if he's still angry, he won't turn us away, surely? The mating pull has to work in our favor, despite my crass words, and the dent you caused."

"He's not going to kick us out. We came back. Just like we said we would." Tugging Ty's hand, Zeke pulled him towards the door, the butterflies in his stomach taking flight. The confidence he was projecting was a ruse. It would be crushing if Daniel had locked them out – a sign that maybe they'd done more damage than they thought to the sheltered young man. "Chin up and smile, so you're always telling me."

Reaching for the door handle, Zeke let out a rush of air as the door opened easily. What was more, the delicious scent of their mate was entwined with something sweet and yummy. *Muffins?* "Hi honey, we're home," he called out as he and Ty went into the living room.

"Come through to the kitchen, I've got coffee for you," Daniel yelled back. Waggling his eyebrows at Ty, Zeke hurried through the house. The fire was roaring away nicely, the lamps Daniel had turned on gave the living room an intimate cozy feel. Soft music was coming from somewhere. *I could get used to this.* But it was the smell Zeke was drawn to and that was coming from the kitchen.

Daniel was standing at the counter, oven gloves on, scooping out fresh baked muffins from a tray onto an already full plate. His cheeks were flushed, and his smile was hesitant, but there was no sign of his earlier anger. "You're just in time. I wasn't sure what you'd like, so I made sweet and savory muffins. The savory ones are bacon and cheese with a hint of chives and the sweet ones are honey, my mom's recipe."

"You did all this in that short time?" Ty beamed. "It looks incredible."

"I wanted to say I was sorry for acting like a brat earlier." Daniel shrugged. "I was so busy being offended, I didn't even stop to consider you were doing something nice for me and probably wanted to spend some time with just the two of you. I mean this has got to be new for you too. Sit down, please."

"Hey," moving quickly around the counter, Zeke grabbed a tea towel and removed the tray from Daniel's hand, before wrapping his arm around his mate's waist. "Yes, we did want to spend a few minutes alone but that was only because we were so damn horny, after seeing you go off like a rocket. We know we'll be your first time, and that can be scary enough for anyone, without having two of us in the mix as well." He leaned over, taking in Daniel's scent. "In case you're wondering, we ended up jacking off. Neither one of us lasted more than two pumps and we were done, and that was all because you got us so riled up."

"I wanted to, you know," Daniel flapped his hand, "return the favor. I just wasn't sure how to go about things."

Ty pulled out a chair and Zeke prodded Daniel over to it, encouraging him to sit. The table was solid wood, painted white. The chairs were made of the same wood and someone had handmade cushion covers for the slightly scooped wooden seats. A rectangle tray, complete with a doily, held the coffee items. Zeke's mom had the same tray and it reminded him of his childhood in a positive way. The smell of the muffins was delicious and for a long moment the men busied themselves pouring coffee and demolishing a few of the baked goods.

"You sure know how to hit the spot with these. They are absolutely delicious," Ty said, swallowing the last of his third muffin. "Now, one hunger's satisfied, we can go back to our sex conversation, because, as we're mates, we do need to clear the air. Firstly, I want to apologize for being an absolute heel. Disappearing on you was a low blow and I never should have opened my mouth. But Zeke put it best when he said we were both ready to blow. After tasting your sweet lips and smelling your spunk, in my head you were already flipped over the back of that couch with your ass bare. It shouldn't be like that for your first time. You deserve sweet loving, not two raging alphas thinking with nothing but their dicks."

Daniel licked the remains of his muffin off his fingers and then picked up his coffee mug. "But you said it yourself, we are mates, you didn't have to make up an excuse to leave. Oh, I get what you're saying, but I still think it would've been kinda hot if you'd have let me watch you get off too."

Zeke, who'd just taken a mouthful of coffee, spluttered it all over the table. Ty and Daniel burst out laughing as he got up and found a dish cloth to clean up his mess. "I'm not usually a barbarian at the table," he said, wiping up the spillage and chucking the dirty cloth into the sink, before sitting down again. "But honestly, you thought it would be hot to watch us?"

Daniel studied his cup. "I'm guessing you guys have been together for a while. You've been used to doing things with just the two of you. It's not going to be easy for you to include me all the time and I understand that. If you'd allow me to watch sometimes... I might learn something."

"Now wait just a minute." Zeke and Ty had talked a thousand times about what life would be like when they found their third. There was never once a mention of them excluding the guy they'd been lucky enough to find. "Ty and I have been together ten years and we've had a lot of fun times together. I'm not going to deny that, or minimize it in any way. We've had an amazing relationship, but there was always something missing and we both knew that. From the moment we scented you, our ten-year-long dreams came true. Once claimed, you'll always be included in all of the things we do – sexy or otherwise."

"We just didn't want to rush you in our first few hours together," Ty explained. "You did swoon on the front door step and all Zeke did was sniff you. We were trying to be considerate, just like you describe in your stories. You wrote something similar once, what it's like when three mates find each other. Oh, what was the book called... um... um...Trouble Comes in Threes, remember that one, Zeke?"

"Silver, Drake and Sebastian." Zeke clicked his fingers. "Their claiming scene was one of the hottest ever and you wrote then about what is was like for an established couple to find their third after so long with just the two of them. You handled that beautifully. And the way Silver and Drake were so gentle with Sebastian's first time – isn't that what you want for yourself?"

"I still can't believe you read my books." Daniel's cheeks were bright red, but he lifted his head and met Zeke's gaze squarely. "A lot of that book was written straight from my hopes and dreams of mating. The research I did for that claiming scene talked about graduating sized butt plugs, and using dildos to help get a virgin ass used to penetration. I placed an online order the day I wrote that initial sex scene and have used them on myself ever since. It took a while to get the hang of inserting the toys by myself, but I've gotten better with practice."

Zeke swallowed hard as a raft of sexy visions of Daniel pleasuring himself filled his brain. "You have a toy collection?" His voice came out as a whisper. He looked across at Ty recognizing the heat in his mate's eyes.

"It's not a collection as such," Daniel said, "but I buy a few items every couple of months to change things up a bit. I wanted to be ready if I ever found my mates."

Zeke knew the question he had to ask, he saw the same question in Ty's eyes. Neither of them wanted to wait anymore. "Daniel," he growled, "are you ready to become our mate? Know that if your answer is yes, we will not be cleaning up the dishes on this table until tomorrow."

Daniel's chest rose and fell and then rose again. It was the longest ten seconds of Zeke's life. "I can live with a messy kitchen table for the night. You two were made for me, the Fates guided you here, so it must be right. Everything else we can work out together. My answer is yes."

His bear roaring triumphantly in his head, Zeke jumped out of his chair, sweeping Daniel in his arms and heading for the stairs, Ty hot on his heels. Daniel's room was easy to find. The bed was a perfect size for three bears to snuggle in. "I've found the lube," Ty yelled, rummaging in the bedside cabinet. Holding up a half used bottle. "It should be enough for tonight at least."

"There's a new bottle in the bathroom cab...." Zeke cut Daniel off. He just had to taste those lips again. He just had to.

Chapter Seven

Ty had always believed there was nothing sexier than watching Zeke when he was horny. The man's eyes would glow, his skin seemed to shimmer with a sense of urgency, even his beard seemed to stiffen up. Being the focus of all that passion was intoxicating and never failed to get Ty's motor running. But seeing him handle Daniel so fucking carefully, while vibrating with need was the hottest thing Ty'd seen yet.

Stripping off, Ty climbed on the bed, where his mates were stretched out, still devouring each other's mouths. Reaching around Daniel's waist, he easily found Daniel's pants button and zipper. He'd love to see Daniel in his full naked glory, but that would have to wait. Zeke's arms wouldn't let him remove Daniel's shirt. The pants, however had to go.

Pushing them down, Daniel had surprisingly long legs, Ty took a moment to run his hands up and down his new mate's thighs. *Such a biteable ass.* But Ty knew if he started touching there, he wouldn't stop. Besides, his big bear would be getting darned uncomfortable in his pants by now. The scent of arousal was already saturating the air and they'd barely started. Brushing a kiss against the small of Daniel's back, Ty groaned at the scent of heat and need coming from his mate. Burying his nose in that tight little crack would be heaven, but he warned himself not to move too fast.

Crawling over sprawled limbs, he made short work of Zeke's pant fastenings. Everything about Daniel was new, but Ty relished the familiarity as he wriggled Zeke out of his jeans, taking a moment to press against his mate's solid back, watching the look of bliss on Daniel's face.

"Let's get the rest of these clothes off," Zeke rasped as he pulled off

Daniel's lips. "It'll be a lot more comfortable."

Lying back on the pillows, his blond hair sprawled about his face, Daniel seemed dazed and unable to speak. Zeke rolled, giving Ty access while he stripped off his top. Ty loved to see Zeke's muscles bunch and flex, but his need to taste Daniel overrode his desire for eye candy. Daniel's skin was smooth and hot to touch as he slid his hands under his new mate's top. "Lift, babe," he said quietly. Daniel pushed up with his arms, grabbing his bunched up top and pulling it over his head.

"You don't have to be gentle," Daniel whispered.

"Maybe I want to be." Still kneeling, Ty bent over, licking Daniel's lips before pressing against them. Daniel was bolder this time, in comparison to their first kiss, smoothing his hands over Ty's torso, exploring hesitantly, although he stayed away from Ty's cock. Ty wasn't in any hurry, although his bear was there – pushing in the background - wanting their cub to wear their mark. *Soon,* he promised.

/~/~/~/~/~/

In all the sex scenes Daniel had imagined, and there'd been dozens of them, nothing prepared him for the feelings stemming from the real thing. Zeke could touch his lips with his own and the simple brush of his facial hair against his chin was enough to send sparks shooting through his cock. Ty had clearly shaved, but he already sporting a five o'clock stubble. And yet his lips were full, and Daniel didn't want to stop sucking them.

Hands, there were hands all over his body, setting his nerves alight in ways he couldn't imagine. It was as if his whole body was an erogenous zone, every where he was touched and licked responded. The hair on Zeke's chest sent tingles up and down his spine as the man worked on prepping him. And that was another fallacy blown. No toy, plastic, silicone or rubber could compare to Zeke's fingers in his ass. His prostate, so hard to find on his own, sung under Zeke's attentions. By the time he found the courage to wrap his fingers around Ty's cock and give an experimental tug, Zeke's hands were on his hips and the blunt head of his cock was pushing for entry.

"You know how to do this, babe," Ty encouraged, pulling back to allow Daniel to breathe. "You've played with toys. You've written about this a hundred times. Just push out."

It's a bit damn different when you're on the receiving end of what feels like an unopened beer can prodding your ass, but just as quickly Daniel's objections fell away. Ty slid down his body and his cock was engulfed in a warm pressure that threatened to make his balls explode in seconds. It wouldn't take much, just a split second more. Daniel always came quickly when he was by himself and apparently it could now be said to be true every time. But then there was a firm tug on his balls and Ty's head started bobbing up and down as Zeke hit home behind him.

Fuck, I forgot about Zeke. The fact he'd been so ably distracted showed how awesome a blow job could be. But Zeke's guttural groan caught Daniel's attention. "Tell me I can move." Zeke sounded as though he was talking through gritted teeth.

"Move?" How the hell was Daniel meant to know when moving was okay. So far, this whole experience had completely blown him away. There was no way he could feel any more amazing than he did right now, not with Ty working his cock as though it was the tastiest lollipop on earth.

And then Zeke proved him wrong. *Thank the Fates for lube,* was all Daniel could think as Zeke rocked in and out. Every pull out tickled the nerve endings around his hole, every in stroke pushed his cock deeper into Ty's mouth who didn't even gag! Daniel felt like he was caught in a whirlpool, suspended by his groin, stimulation hitting him from all angles and all he could do was hang onto Ty's shoulders and let the sensations flow through his body like a wave.

Lying on his side, Daniel turned his head easily when Zeke fingers latched in his hair, tilting his neck, offering his throat. He knew what was coming, so did his bear. Zeke's thrusts got harder and faster and Daniel closed his eyes. His orgasm, which felt like it'd been building forever, was right there again, the urge getting stronger and stronger and then Zeke struck. One split second of pain against his neck, and then bliss washed over his body, infusing his mind and making him whole. Zeke was everywhere – in his head, in his body, and as his bear spirit rose to meet the older Kodiak, their joining resonated in his very soul. It was perfect, it was everything Daniel could possibly imagine and more. He barely noticed Ty had pulled off his softening dick until the man wiped the saliva off his lips and said, "my turn."

/~/~/~/~/

Zeke flopped back on the mattress, his chest heaving, his dick a sticky mess. He knew he should get up and get a cloth, but damn, he just wanted to savor the after glow for a moment. Claiming Ty had been a clash of alphas, with struggles for dominance and Ty giving as good as he got. With Daniel, it was so different and yet just as intense. Zeke knew he'd already lost his heart to his little cutie and they hadn't even known each other a day. He just hoped that given time, Daniel would come to feel the same way real soon.

The only thing that was missing, apart from a handy washcloth, was Daniel's mark on his neck. He guessed Daniel had been taught omegas didn't do that to their alphas, but Zeke wasn't the type who thought wearing an omega mark made him weak. That was alpha bullshit as far as he was concerned, and he knew Ty felt the same. It was something they would have to talk about, later, after a clean up and a sleep.

Rolling over onto his side, Zeke felt his cock stiffen again as he watched Ty thrusting hard into their younger mate who was groaning up a storm. It was Zeke's fault Ty didn't get to top very often. It wasn't that he didn't switch, it's just he didn't do it often. He would bottom for Daniel too though, even if it was just so the sweet cub could experience what it was like and to cement their claim. He stroked the bare patch on his neck where Daniel's claiming mark would go and smirked. That would be an interesting night.

Reaching out, he ran his hand over Ty's flexing ass, kneading the flesh, grazing Ty's hole with his finger. Ty roared and slammed into Daniel one last time, the faint scent of blood and Ty's spunk letting Zeke know their cub was now double marked.

"You're an asshole, you know that?" Ty said when he pulled his teeth free, panting hard, his cock still buried deep in their cub's body. "I was trying to make it last. You only get one first time with a new mate."

"I think you did enough," Zeke's grin widened as he nodded at Daniel. The sweet man was sprawled out, eyes closed, mouth slack, gently snoring, even though Ty was still inside of him. "You've worn our cub out."

"His stamina will improve the longer we're together," Ty said fondly, carefully pulling out his cock and reaching for the blankets. "If I recall, we were both worn out when we first met."

"And that motel shower was far too piddly to take both of us," Zeke remembered. "Come on, let's see if

Daniel's is any better and find him a washcloth. As much as it's really hot seeing our spunk leaking out of that cute puffy ass, he'll be really uncomfortable when he wakes up."

"We did it," Ty leaned over kissing Zeke softly. "We found our cub. Now we've got a whole new chapter of our lives to start, all three of us together."

"We've made a good start."

Chapter Eight

Five days later and Ty was getting used to his and Zeke's new lifestyle. The three men had settled into a relaxed routine, lazing in bed in the morning, having an early brunch, then Daniel would insist he had to work. Zeke and Ty split their time between catching up on their own businesses online and exploring the property. Six o'clock, they'd all meet for dinner and spend the evening watching movies and getting to know each other more.

Daniel seemed fascinated by some of the funnier stories they had to share, although he offered little from his own life. Probably, because he spent most of his adult years alone, something both Zeke and Ty felt was incredibly sad and an issue they wanted to do something about. Unfortunately, trying to talk to Daniel about branching out more, and seeing new things proved a sticking point.

Today was a classic example. It all started innocently enough at the kitchen table over brunch.

"That was delicious, thank you Ty," Zeke said, pushing his plate away. "I was thinking, we should all take a ride into town this morning. The cupboards are looking bare, and we ate the last of the steak for dinner last night. What do you think, cub? Can you stand to be away from your laptop for one day? We could get some lunch, see a bit of the town while we're at it. Make a real day of it."

"You guys can go." Daniel seemed to find his last piece of toast fascinating. "I'm in the middle of a huge scene. I should get back to it."

"It will still be there tomorrow." Ty really wanted to take Daniel out. Apart from picking up their gear from the B&B, he and Zeke hadn't left the property. "I know your writing's important, sweetie, but some fresh air will do you good. Surely one day off won't hurt?"

"I'm not sure how we could all travel together." Avoiding Ty's gaze, Daniel got up, collecting the plates and taking them over to the sink to rinse. "My car's not big enough to take all three of us and the groceries, and I don't want to upset either one of you by riding with one and not the other. It would be better if you two went. I'll be fine."

"That's not how a mating works, cub." Zeke was getting frustrated – Ty could tell from his tone. He never did well, staying in one place all the time. Zeke was a doing person. "We can't stay holed up in this house forever. For one thing, we'd starve. What's the harm in going out and having a bit of fun."

"I know it must be boring for you, but I explained the morning after our claiming my work is important to me." Turning, Daniel leaned against the sink, his arms folded across his chest. Ty got a sinking feeling in his belly. "I don't expect you two to sit around here all day waiting for me to finish my latest scene. I don't have a problem with you going out whenever you want. Just don't expect me to go today."

"Why not?" Zeke demanded. "We're mates. Your bear wants to be with us, as much as we want you. The world isn't going to stop if you take one day away from your work."

Shit, that was the wrong thing to say. The sinking feeling in Ty's stomach turned into a black hole. Daniel straightened, his lips tight. "Babe," Ty said quickly. "We never got a chance to take you out before the claiming. Don't you want to come on a date with us?"

"A date?" Daniel made it sound like it was a foreign word and Ty caught a hint of vulnerability in his young mate. But then, just as quickly it was gone. "You know I care about you both a great deal, but my story is at an important stage right now. We can talk about this after it's finished."

"You said last night that could take at least another week, and that's without editing and everything else," Zeke roared. "I told you when we mated, we'd do everything together. Ty and I were never apart in ten years and that's the way it should be between mates. Is your story really more important than spending time with us doing something fun for a change?"

"My writing is fun for me. It's also how I make my living. I have readers waiting for this story."

For the first time since they got together, tempers were flaring. Ty tried once again to diffuse the situation. "Babe, Zeke wasn't suggesting what you do wasn't important, but surely spending a day out will help clear your head, maybe even give you new ideas to work into your plot?"

"Oh yes, because grocery shopping is a really crucial part of my plot," Daniel snapped.

"Hey, you don't get to talk to Ty like that." Ty's heart warmed at Zeke's defense, but it wasn't helping, and neither was what he said next. "It's not as though you have a publisher, or a deadline except the one in your own head."

Daniel blew out a long breath, his fists clenched. "Thank you for so succinctly implying my work isn't good enough for a publisher. For your information, I make far more money as a self-published author than I ever would with a traditional publisher. And while I might not have an editor or someone pushing me for a deadline, I do have people online who are waiting for this story. I will not let them down just because you're bored. If you don't want to be sitting around here while I'm working, then go out, the pair of you."

"That's not what I meant, and you know it," Zeke said hotly. "I want you to come with us. Isn't that important to you either?"

"You want, you want. What about what I want?" Ty cringed as Daniel's voice rose. "The pair of you tracked me down and moved yourselves in as though you owned the place and I accepted all of that gladly. But I knew my lifestyle would be too dull and boring for you, and could've told you that before you claimed me. Well, you did claim me, and now you're stuck with me. But if you think I'm going to let some geriatric Kodiak think he can boss me around and pull me away from something I feel is important just because he said so, you've got another thing coming." Storming off towards the office, both men jumped as the door slammed and the unmistakable sound of a lock being turned rang through their ears.

"I guess he doesn't want to go out then," Ty said eventually when the silence became overwhelming. "We can't force him to go if he doesn't want to."

"I'm beginning to think there's something unnatural about that cub of ours," Zeke was still fuming. "Why doesn't he want to come with us? Is he ashamed of being seen with us?"

"I don't think that's it, babe." At least Ty hoped that wasn't it. "I think he's just got a touch of social anxiety, that's all."

"If he'd bite the pair of us, then we'd be able to read his freaking mind and know what was going on with him." Ty knew how much Daniel's refusal to claim them hurt the older man. Not that Daniel came right out and said "no" specifically, it was just any time Ty or Zeke brought up the idea of him having a go at topping for a change, Daniel either stuck his ass in the air or bent down and wrapped his lips around the nearest dick. *He's getting remarkably good at deflection,* Ty thought wryly.

"I'm hoping he's just feeling overwhelmed right now," Ty offered. "It can't be easy, living your life entirely on your own for so long and then suddenly accepting instant changes. Not everyone reacts to change very well."

"I want to show him off," Zeke frowned.

"Just like you did me," Ty remembered. "He's not an alpha, maybe he doesn't have those feelings."

"Any omega I met before you, couldn't wait to be seen on my arm." Zeke ran his hand over his head. "Fuck it. What are we going to do? It's not as though we can go out now, after all that's been said. He'll think we don't want him."

"We could just go and get the groceries and come back." Ty looked down the short hallway to where Daniel's office was. "I don't feel right about leaving though."

"You think there's something going on with him, we don't know about yet?"

Ty nodded. "He's scared of something, but I doubt it's got anything to do with any external threat. There's something going on in his head. Maybe he doesn't know how to explain. Maybe he doesn't want to upset us."

"He didn't have any problems calling me a geriatric. Fuck, I'm only a hundred and forty three, it's not as though I've even hit middle age yet."

"When you're twenty, anyone over thirty five is middle-aged," Ty chuckled. "He was upset, you know he didn't mean it."

Zeke sighed. "That doesn't help our empty cupboard situation. I suppose out of the two of us, I'd better go and do the grocery run. You'd be far better at talking to him than I would when he comes out."

"And you need a good ride to clear your head. I understand," Ty managed a small smile. "I'm not going to ruin my manhood card by saying I'll miss you, but don't take too long, yeah?"

Pushing back his chair, Zeke pulled Ty from his, onto his lap. "I don't like being away from either one of you, but someone has to go out and hunt."

"Pushing a cart around a supermarket is hardly hunting," Ty nibbled along Zeke's ear. "I'll board up the fortress and protect the cub."

"You know, if this had happened even fifty years ago, I'd have slung that cub over my shoulder and carried him off and there'd be nothing anyone would say about it."

"In the shifter world maybe, but in the human world, kidnapping was always an offense," Ty reminded softly. "Just because you long for the good old days when us bears lived in log huts, and hunted for all we could eat, I don't. I quite like our creature comforts, thank you very much."

"Daniel wouldn't have been spending all his time on the computer if he lived back then," Zeke grumbled. "He wouldn't have had the internet for a start." He waggled his eyebrows. "That's an idea. Do you think he'd come out if we cut a few wires to his modem?"

"No, I don't. He'd probably have a complete meltdown," Ty laughed. "Go on, my geriatric Kodiak. Go get food. Ride safe."

"Always." Zeke's toe curling kiss didn't completely wipe out the ache in Ty's insides, but it helped.

Chapter Nine

Daniel wiggled in his chair, the needs of his bladder getting more and more insistent. For all he'd said to his mates about the importance of his next scene, he hadn't written a word since he heard the bike take off an hour before. He stayed shut in his office though, terrified of the reception he'd get when his men returned. *If they returned.* The little voice in the back of his head had been just as insistent as his bladder, leading Daniel to worry he'd pushed his mate's too far this time.

"Fuck, I'm such an idiot." Daniel buried his face in his hands. "It's not as though I can stay in here all day." The problem was, he couldn't explain to his mates why he didn't want to go out. Anything he said would reinforce the image that he was nothing more than a child. *They probably think that any way – storming off like a toddler who's been refused a snack five minutes before dinner time.*

The issues stemmed from his own insecurities. Daniel knew that. But that didn't mean he could explain them to anyone else, so they'd understand. He sucked at that sort of thing, which didn't help the insecurity aspect. *And it doesn't help that I really, really, really need to pee.* Straining his ears, he couldn't hear the remotest sound of a bike engine. *I'll be quick.* Daniel knew he wasn't ready to face his mates yet.

Unlocking the office door, Daniel shot down the hallway into the small half-bath he had installed on the ground floor. Not even bothering to close the door, he unzipped his pants and let out a sigh of relief. *So much better.* Finishing up, he washed his hands, dried them on the hand towel, turned and squeaked. Well, he was a bear so he wouldn't admit to a squeak, but a definite "eep" left his lips. Ty was standing in the hallway, his arms folded across his chest and a decided lack of expression on his handsome face.

"I… er… I thought you'd gone out with Zeke." *Why did I have to get caught in the toilet? No one can look cool or like they know what they are doing in a bathroom, damn it.*

"I know what you thought, cub. Are you going to stand in the bathroom all day, or shall we sit in the living room and talk about what happened this morning like adults?"

And yeah, Ty really isn't happy with me. Daniel went for a casual tone. "I don't know what we have to talk about. You wanted to go out, I didn't. End of story."

"Interesting use of the word story." Ty quirked an eyebrow. "The excuse you use to get out of anything outside of your comfort zone. But it is just an excuse, isn't it? You haven't typed a word all day."

How did he? …damn, the lack of key clacks. Daniel stuck out his chin. "I don't ask you what you and Zeke get up to all day when I'm busy. Hell, I

116

don't even know how you make a living. So, you don't have the right to criticize me just because your keen ears didn't pick up the sound of my keyboard being used. I could have been handwriting for all you know, plotting out the next scene."

"Were you?" Ty's expression dared him to lie, which Daniel would never do. But the fact Ty thought he might made Daniel's heart sink.

"No." Daniel looked anywhere that Ty wasn't. "I felt bad about what I said, and couldn't concentrate. Happy now?"

"No. I'm not happy with any of this."

Ouch, Daniel had never heard Ty be so blunt before. He'd always been the caring one.

"Zeke is out alone, getting groceries because we needed them, and I'd far rather we were with him, instead of having this conversation in the hallway. But someone needs to get a handle on the shit you're not telling us, and I was nominated for the job."

"I don't need handling," Daniel cried, stung his older and more confident mates had so little faith in him. "I just don't like going out. I'm not good with people face to face."

"You could've said that, instead of insulting our other mate and running off to lock yourself in the office." Ty's voice softened. "Are you ashamed to be seen with us? Is that it?"

"No." So busy with the crap in his own head, Daniel hadn't even considered how his mates viewed his mini rant. "You two are fine looking men. Anyone would be proud to be seen out with you."

"Then why aren't you?"

It was a reasonable question, but Daniel wasn't sure he could answer. But he opened his mouth anyway. He had to try. Ty let Zeke go out alone because of him which wasn't fair to either of them. Bears were notorious for going from being solitary when they were unmated, to damn near living in each other's pockets when they were. Ty and Zeke were a classic example. "How would it work, the three of us together in public? It was fine when it was just you and Zeke. You two could handle any homophobes you came across, you're both big enough to look after yourselves. But what happens when you throw a third in the mix? Me? Do we just go out as friends, or what? I don't get it. I've never seen a relationship like ours. What will people think?"

"They can think what they like." Ty shrugged. "It's not as though me or Zeke are going to molest you in a diner somewhere. We do know how to act in public and around humans. We've been doing it for long enough."

"I can control myself around humans," Daniel slapped his hand against his own chest. "But I've never been on a date before. I don't know how to act, or what to say. Is handholding acceptable, or do I have to keep my hands in my pockets? Does one of us pay for everyone's meal, or do we each pay for ourselves? Is it okay to use pet names in public, or will that cause a fight with bigots? I mean, we're mates, we know that, but people out in the real world don't even understand the concept. What happens if someone says something nasty, and then you and Zeke will get all protective, and someone could get hurt. You could get hurt. Shit, you could even be arrested for all I know. But that's just it. I don't know. The only thing I know is that I don't want anything to happen to either one of you."

"Oh, babe, all that worry in that busy head of yours." Stepping closer, Ty pulled him to his chest, somewhere Daniel was happy to be. The scent of his mates always soothed him, among other things. "Why didn't you say something instead of getting upset and storming off?"

"I didn't know how." Daniel nuzzled into Ty's chest, his hands slipping easily around the bigger man's waist. "I have enough trouble with social interaction as it is. Zeke was saying only last night about your last year's trip to that festival you're missing this week. How you met up with a whole bunch of people, and had so much fun, arm wrestling and dancing. I can't do anything like that. My face goes beet red and my hands get sweaty if someone asks me my name."

"That's why Zeke suggested lunch out in town first," Ty dropped a kiss on Daniel's head but didn't take things any further, which was a pity in Daniel's opinion. "We know you haven't had a lot of chance in experiencing life, but think how awesome it would be if you were making memories with us."

"I wish I had your confidence," Daniel sighed. "I got an email this morning asking me to confirm I'd be going to the MM Romance convention in Roswell next week. I've been asked to be one of the guest speakers and participate on a panel, so readers can ask me questions."

"Sounds like something we could all go to."

"I wish. I've dreamed about how wonderful it could be, meeting fellow authors, interacting with people who love my characters as much as I do. Before you guys came, I used to spend hours imagining the witty things I'd say, and how amazing it would be to meet some of the people I've chatted with online in person. But I will probably have a sprained ankle or a bad case of the flu again, like last year."

"That's not nice little bear, bears don't get the flu," Ty chided. "I bet all your fans get excited to see you and then you don't show up."

"How can I?" Daniel had had enough of standing in the hallway. Reaching behind him to take Ty's hand, he led him towards the kitchen. "When people realize what an absolute bore I am, they'll stop buying my books. Or worse, I'll be sitting on the panel and someone will actually ask me something, if they even turn up for the Q&A session, and my throat will close up, I'll take a sip of water and probably end up squirting it out of my nose as I choke on it. I'll be a laughing stock."

Kitchen. Coffee. Dropping Ty's hand, Daniel reached for his mug and then remembered he'd left it in the office. No matter, he could drink out of any mug and Ty would probably want one too. He busied himself making two cups, taking care to ensure Ty's was just how he liked it – not too strong, a dash of milk and four spoonfuls of sugar.

Ty waited until Daniel was seated and they both had mugs in their hands before asking, "Is that the worst thing you think could happen if we all went to this conference thing of yours – people will laugh at you?"

"No." Daniel was completely serious. He'd given it a lot of thought. "I don't know how to get there for a start. My luggage could get stolen, the hotel might have double booked my room, so I'd have nowhere to stay. I'd get lost in a strange town and I'm not sure I could write in a new place, so my new release would be late. The food could be horrible, I could get abducted by aliens. The conference is in Roswell, you know."

"I'm sure if aliens tried to abduct you, they'd be in for a hell of a shock," Ty's lips twitched. Daniel frowned. He had a suspicion his mate wasn't taking his concerns seriously. Ty must have seen his expression, because he went on.

"Getting there wouldn't be a problem because we'd take you on the bikes. Hotel rooms are locked so your luggage will be fine. We'll make sure to get to the hotel early enough, so you don't lose your booking, and you won't get lost because you know how to use Google maps and we'll be with you. If the food is that bad in the hotel, we can find a McDonalds, Subway, or Wendy's and live off burgers for a few days. As for writing, I'm sure if your online followers actually knew you were going to a convention, they'd be so thrilled to see you, they wouldn't mind if your book release was late. You could treat it like a holiday."

"A holiday," Daniel gulped. That concept was just as anxiety causing as the "date" word.

"We'd be with you," Ty promised. "We won't leave your side for a second. You could pretend we're your two sexy bodyguards, if you're uncomfortable with people knowing we're mates."

"My readers think mates are just in fantasy stories." Daniel was torn between anticipation and gut numbing fear. "I don't have a relationship status on my social media profiles. I didn't want anyone to say I was in a fake relationship to boost sales of my books. In fact, I don't say a lot about myself or my life at all online."

"That's so much better," Ty grinned. "You'll be the mysterious D.B. Bear, complete with a biker entourage. And if Z and me play the part of bodyguards, then no one will be surprised if we're overly protective."

"It's for three whole days and that's without travel time." *Around hundreds of people.*

"Even better. We'll take a week off, and make a real fun trip out of it."

Could I really do this? It all sounded so easy when Ty talked about it. Daniel tilted his head as he heard Zeke's bike in the driveway. "I'll make Zeke a coffee," he said, getting up and heading to the pot. But Ty pulled at the back of his shirt and lightly pushed him in the other direction.

"I'll make the coffee, you go and tell Zeke we're going to Roswell."

Chapter Ten

Zeke barely got the bike stopped and resting on its kickstand, when Daniel was scrambling onto the bike, pushing into his arms, peppering tiny kisses along his beard line. "I'm sorry, I'm sorry," Daniel whispered. "I didn't mean to call you a geriatric. I really, really care about you, so much. Can you ever forgive me?"

Considering Zeke was happy enough Daniel was talking to them again, forgiving him for a few harsh words wasn't going to be an issue. The bike ride helped clear his head, just as Ty suggested. During the ride, Zeke reminded himself Daniel was young, and Ty's words about something bothering their cub hit home as soon as he stopped fuming about the geriatric comment. By the time he'd turned into the driveway Zeke was ready to be home and in the arms of his mates.

"Nothing to forgive, my cub." Zeke held on tight, tugging Daniel's feet off the ground. His mate smelled of jasmine and musk, just like he always did, with heady undertones of arousal and... and... *excitement? Nerves?* Zeke couldn't be sure. "Did you have a talk to Ty?"

"Yep," Daniel moved over to suckle Zeke's earlobe. A shiver ran right down his chest and high-fived his growing dick.

"And?" Standing, Daniel still in his arms, Zeke swung his leg over the bike and headed for the porch where Ty was leaning against the doorframe, holding two mugs. Daniel noticed him too and the red on his cheeks darkened.

"How would you like to be my guests at an MM Romance convention in Roswell next week? Ty thought you two could go as my bodyguards or entourage or something." Daniel's words were rushed, and it took a moment for them to sink in.

"A road trip to Roswell?" Zeke grinned, looking over at Ty, who winked. "Best idea ever. Let's go to bed and celebrate with a fuck."

"After Daniel's made the changes to the hotel bookings, and confirmed by email he'll be one of the guest speakers and participate in the Q&A," Ty said firmly.

"You're going to be a guest speaker at this conference thing? Yee hah," Zeke swung Daniel around. "It's going to be so hot, standing in the background, watching you give your speech. I can't wait."

"Oh my god, the speech. I didn't expect to have to write one." Daniel scrambled out of his arms and went running into the house. Moments later, a door slammed.

"Damn," Zeke nudged his cock into a more comfortable position, before reaching for the coffee mug Ty handed him. "I was looking forward to that fuck too."

"You had two last night. You can wait a few more hours for another one. Come and sit down, big guy. Did you arrange for the food to be delivered?" Zeke followed Ty over to the large porch swing and sat with him shoulder-to shoulder, staring out over the view.

"Yeah, I ordered double of everything, which could be a waste if we're going away. But hell, most of it will freeze. Want to tell me how you got Daniel to go from refusing to go out on a simple lunch date, to getting him to agree to attend a conference?"

"A bit of patience, a wee nudge here and there, but I was right. That boy has a whole crate of worries in his head." Zeke listened as Ty explained about the fears Daniel had of going out period. His worries about how to act on a date, the things he got upset about just thinking about attending a conference where he was honored with being a guest speaker.

"Are all these worries because he doesn't trust us to look after him, do you think?" Zeke asked when Ty had finished.

"I don't think that's a conscious concern," Putting down his mug, Ty slid his hand into Zeke's. "It's more he hasn't had anyone to rely on before, and he's not sure how."

"Losing his parents must have been one hell of a shock," Zeke said thinking about his cub's past. "You think about it. He'd have been all full of new shifter hormones and puberty at the time. He's never said anything negative about his parents, so they must have been good to him. Imagine having that sort of safety net ripped away without warning, at such a crucial part of his development."

"And then being shoved into a human foster care system, while still trying to cope with his new bear form." Ty leaned his head on Zeke's shoulder. "I can't even imagine what that must have been like. Admittedly, Daniel's an omega, but even so, his bear's need to lash out, come out, and probably terrify the others in the foster home must have been devilishly hard for our mate to control."

"He said he buried himself in books, remember?" Zeke remembered talking about where his love of reading came from. "But even so, to be so crippled with anxiety he barely goes out at all." He looked around at the solidly built house. "You can see why this place is important to him."

"His safe place." Ty smiled. "Our cub chose well. This is a beautiful area for bears."

Leaning back on the swing, Zeke raised his boot against the porch rail to start them rocking gently. "I'm thinking, and don't do the shock horror thing because I know you don't think I do it very often...."

Ty chuckled, his head warm on Zeke's shoulder.

"But I'm thinking that this trip is exactly what we all need to cement our relationship." Zeke let out a long breath. "I know I don't do this mushy stuff very often, but I really care about our cub. But you heard what he said, he doesn't even know how we support ourselves."

"He's never asked, and we never offered the information," Ty agreed. "But in all fairness, he spends most of his day locked up in that office of his, or in bed with us. I guessed that was why you suggested lunch today, as a way to break what is becoming a rut."

"A rut for us, a safe routine for him. It's damn hard thinking of anything mundane when that little sweetie pushes his ass into my lap." Zeke took a sip of his coffee and then put the mug on the porch. It'd gone cold. "The Fates put him in our path for a reason, but sometimes it's hard to see why. We've made a life out of traveling the past ten years. He's hunkered down into permanent hibernation – his only friends are on his computer."

"That's because it's never been safe for him to find face-to-face friends," Ty said. "Can you imagine what he looked like at fifteen? A blond haired waif with 'bully me' in neon lights above his head. No wonder he spent all his time lost in a fictional world. You keep forgetting," Ty's shoulder nudged Zeke's, "Daniel's an omega. He's not hard wired to fight back."

Zeke's hands curled into claws, the idea of his cute cub being bullied enough to rouse his bear, even if it was years before. "We have to be his safe place," he growled. "We'll show we can protect him. He just has to trust us."

"Which is why we have to get him out of the house," Ty reminded him quietly. "Daniel needs to gain his confidence and the only way he can do that is by stepping out of his comfort zone and realizing we're there to make things easier for him."

Ty was right. Zeke knew he was right, but that still didn't stop him from wanting to rip the throat out of any passing bully. A tree might have to work as a substitute for living flesh. "I need...."

"What you need is to sheath those claws and use your anger energy to help me carry in the groceries which are on their way up the driveway. Then you can help me cook our mate a lovely meal, and afterwards, we'll sit down and talk like grownups and share some of the important details with our mate, like how many assets we own, how much money we have and where it all comes from. Then hopefully, he won't be so insistent on working every day when he sees he's actually a rich man."

"You know I'm going to want to sink my cock into him the moment he sits on my lap," Zeke grumbled. He couldn't help it. He was a man of simple tastes.

"Well as the only sounds that come out of your mouth are grunts and roars when you're rutting, keep your pants buttoned up until after we've talked." Ty stood and stretched. "It'll be damn good to get on the road again, especially now we actually have a home to come home to."

"We've got to get Daniel on the back of our bikes first." Even though Zeke knew in his gut the trip would be good for all of them, his instinct also told him Daniel was going to try on a mountain of excuses before they hit the road.

Chapter Eleven

"Just remember, hold onto my waist, and don't fight me when I lean." Three days of mad panic, and they were finally ready to leave. Ty made sure Daniel's jacket collar was snug against his neck and then climbed on his bike. Zeke was already waiting on his.

"I'm not sure if I locked the front door," Daniel made to go back up the porch stairs.

"You've checked it twice. Climb on."

"What about the back door? Did anyone..."

"Double checked," Zeke called out. "Not even an ant could get in the back door."

"The power," Daniel cried. "We can't leave that...."

"All the fuses are pulled except for the one for the freezer," Ty said. "Now get on. My stomach is already grumbling, and we've got an hour's ride before we can stop for food."

"We could have lunch here." Daniel latched onto that idea like a pit-bull and Ty sighed. It'd been like that most of the morning – most of the past three days actually. Firstly, there'd been the swag issue – Daniel didn't have any and apparently, he needed it to give out to readers. A superfast order online took care of that, along with delivery instructions to send them directly to where the conference was being held.

Then there was the hotel. Worried sick the hotel would double book their room, Daniel tried getting a backup booking in a neighboring hotel, but they didn't have custom king beds. Daniel had a meltdown. Clothes, Daniel wasn't sure what to wear. The conference's eighties theme party caused another meltdown, until Zeke pointed out that leather jackets, jeans and a white t-shirt hadn't been out of style since the fifties. A rush order secured the snug fitting leather jacket Daniel was wearing.

Packing, books to take, room in the saddle bags for Daniel's computer. Then he fretted about how secure the house would be while they were gone. The fridge had to be emptied out and Daniel insisted on changing the sheets on the bed and *doing the damn laundry*. Zeke spent a lot of time running his hand over his head and Ty was in danger of becoming as bald as his bigger mate.

Letting a long calming breath out, Ty kept his voice low. "Get on the bike, Daniel, I won't let you fall."

One last longing look at the house and then Daniel's shoulders slumped. Lifting his leg, he slid over the pillion seat as Ty had shown him thirty minutes before, settling his feet on the peddles. "Don't panic," Ty yelled as he and Zeke started their bikes and the engines roared, "and hang on."

Clicking the bike into gear, Ty felt Daniel's grip tighten as the bike started to move down the driveway. Looking across at Zeke, Ty grinned and winked at Zeke's thumbs up. His stress headache was easing already.

/~/~/~/~/

What the hell am I doing? The fluttering butterflies in Daniel's stomach hadn't eased at all an hour into their trip. He'd got a handle on being a pillion passenger on the bike fairly quickly, although he knew Ty and Zeke were taking things easy on him. He knew the plan – Zeke had mapped out every one of their stops for him the day before. The experienced bikers decided no more than two hours riding without a break – apparently Daniel's butt would appreciate the stops. He knew where they were staying and when, and how they were going to get there. But that didn't stop his freak out.

My house, my story. I should be writing. Not that Daniel had been able to concentrate when he was given time to write. And he knew it was all his fault. To hear Ty and Zeke talk about their trips, they normally just packed a change of clothes, got on their bikes and went. They just went – no planning, only a vague idea of a destination. What was worse, the two big bears thrived on that sort of thing. Zeke'd laughed when Daniel asked if they ever worried they wouldn't find a place to stay. *A bear can shit in the woods,* he remembered Zeke saying, *and sleep in them too if necessary, although it doesn't pay to do those two things in the same place.* And then he laughed, like the idea of having hotel or motel bookings was a foreign concept.

They're a foreign concept to me too, Daniel thought glumly, tightening his grip as Ty leaned. He was too short to see over Ty's shoulder, which didn't help his nerves, although the rumble of the bike was pleasant once he got used to it. But he was still fretting. His one stint at sleeping outside had been years before, back when he first went into foster care. It was not one of his happier memories.

It was going to take them two days to get to Roswell. That meant two nights where motel bookings could get lost or ignored. Two days having to rely on questionable food choices at roadside diners. Daniel read reviews – he'd seen the horror stories of people's experiences online. Ty and Zeke brushed off his concerns like they were nothing.

I should've claimed my mates when they asked me to. That thought crept unbidden into the forefront of his mind, like it'd been doing since it was brought up the second night his mates were with him and the offer was made. Daniel was well versed on mating habits, in theory anyway. Double claimed bears had a mind link, although in Ty and Zeke's case, they didn't get one, which is how they knew from the start of their relationship they were meant for a third. Sitting on the back of a bike, the only one of the three wearing a helmet at his mates' insistence, talking was impossible over the sound of the engines. Which meant Daniel was alone with his thoughts. *Having a mind link would come in real handy right now.*

The scenery flashing past, Daniel thought back to the night he'd met his mates. His father's voice – *are you going to let your fears define you?* He'd pushed past his fear then, opened the door to his house and two bears moved in. But for Daniel it seemed like his fears multiplied with every passing day. Fear of not being good enough, fear his mates would tire of him, fear of leaving the house, fear of being on this damn trip going to a damn conference where he was going to have to give a speech. *Fear of claiming my mates in case my inexperience hurts them.*

Daniel was so tired of being scared, anxious, and worried all the time. In his house, he had his daily routine, and that calmed him to a certain extent. In just over a week, his two bear mates had stomped all over his routine and pushed him well past any comfort zone he had. And now he was going on a road trip, to a new place, with new people, and... and... and....

Ty was slowing the bike down. *What's happening? Is something wrong?* But no, out to the side, Daniel could see a large truck stop sign. Unsure if he could eat, Daniel knew he had to try, otherwise his mates would worry about him. *Let's try facing these fears one at a fucking time,* he thought, inhaling sharply as the bike came to a stop.

Chapter Twelve

Zeke grinned as he bumped shoulders with Ty, heading into the truck stop. While he was learning to re-appreciate the benefits of a home base, being on the road was in his blood. He and Ty had passed through the area a few years before and had stopped at this very truck stop, although looking around, nothing had changed. The tables gleamed, the counter was lined with a row of bar stools, about half of them empty, and the smell of beef stew and bacon hit his nostrils. His eyes lit up as he saw a grizzled face much like his own at the counter.

"Mortimer, you old sod, fancy bumping into you here. Look, babe, it's my brother." Leaving Ty and Daniel, Zeke hurried forward to meet him.

"Z." Mortimer stood up, chest and fist bumping his sibling. His eyes twinkled, and Zeke knew he'd spotted Ty and Daniel. "Adding to the clan, I see," he chuckled. "Has all that traveling paid off for you at last?"

Zeke was pleased to see his older brother and not just because he wanted to show off Daniel. Ty had met Mortimer a half a dozen times through the years, and while Mortimer preferred his solitary existence, their bears could all get along long enough to be thrown out of a few bars, and rumble with a few locals at different places. Like Zeke, Mortimer shaved his head and his beard was a good three inches longer than his own, something Zeke secretly envied. But he'd never say so – Mortimer's ego was big enough.

"We've found our home, bro," he whispered, leaning in close to Mortimer's ear. "Put a smile on, our new cub is shy." Stepping back, he said in his more normal tone, "Ty, you already know my brother." Ty and Morty exchanged nods and a smile. "Daniel, this is Mortimer, he's older than me by about three years and never lets me forget it. Morty, dust off the manners our mama drummed into our heads, this is Daniel, also known as the author D.B. Bear."

"Good looks and brains," Mortimer teased. "Daniel, it's a pleasure. If you've heard anything about me, I assure you it's all lies."

"I haven't known these guys long." Daniel blushed and ducked his head, tilting it slightly.

"It's our first road trip together," Zeke said happily, knowing Mortimer would understand from that just how new their relationship was. "Daniel's a guest speaker at a conference in Roswell. We thought we'd take our time getting there and have some fun along the way."

"You guys probably want to catch up for a bit," Ty said, with a warm smile at Mortimer. "Daniel and I will snag a table and put in an order. Come and join us when you're ready."

"Nice to meet you," Daniel said shyly as he scurried away. Mortimer whistled under his breath, watching Daniel's ass move in his jeans.

"Did you hit the jackpot or what? First you snag that hunky Ty and now you've added a sweet cub to the mix."

Zeke growled but there was no heat in it. Plopping into the bar stool next to Mortimer's seat, he turned over his cup to show he wanted coffee. The cup was quickly filled but the waitress didn't linger. "Our cub's not without issues, bro, but definitely worth the effort."

"He's seems shy, nothing at all like Ty." Mortimer sat back down, there was a half-eaten plate of pancakes in front of his place.

"He's a bit of a hermit," Zeke confided quietly. "Parental accident when he was fifteen. No family to claim him. Went into the foster system."

"Oh, fuck no, really?" Mortimer shook his head, his eyes sad. "It's the one failing of our kind, bro. Too few extended families, precious few clans. He's not the first I've met who fell through the cracks and was expected to cope alone although," he looked around, but no one was paying attention, "definitely the first omega I've heard of though. That's a huge fucking shame."

"Ty and I have talked about that." Zeke checked over his shoulder, but his mates were across the room. "We figure either his parents died before he presented, or they knew but either thought they were invincible, or they didn't have anyone to call on if something did happen to them and were trusting they'd be around until Daniel was an adult."

"That type of history explains why he's looking like someone's going to jump on him without warning." Zeke realized Morty was watching his mates through the huge mirror that ran at the back of the serving area. "Our teens don't belong in a government system. So, where's this home of yours?"

"A tiny place called Edendale. Fancy coming to visit?" Zeke was pleased.

"I figure someone has to report back to mom. You're the only one established so far, you know that?"

"Didn't Susie and Sarah...?" Zeke thought his sisters were mated. Although it had been at least four years since he'd seen them.

"Bonded." Mortimer spat the word. "Their hormones hit them hard, they wanted cubs of their own so they up and bonded with a pair of brothers who turned out to be right assholes." Mortimer stabbed his last pancake with his knife and shoved it in his mouth.

Zeke grinned. "I take it, the assholes had a visit from big brother?"

"You'd better believe it." Morty chewed noisily and swallowed hard. "They were last seen running over Bear Mountain, clutching where their balls used to be. The sisters are back with mom, determined to wait for the right people this time."

"What about you?" Zeke looked his brother up and down. "The only thing different I can see is your facial hair's in danger of being caught in your belt buckle."

"Jealous much?" Mortimer ran his fingers down his beard and smirked. "Still looking. Nothing promising yet. Mom holds you up as the gold standard. She adores Ty, as you know. She's going to have kittens when she finds out about Daniel."

"Jealous much?" Zeke nudged his brother. "Come on, let's go and sit with them. Daniel's probably already planning his escape. He really didn't want to make this trip."

"Ah, Ty's persuasive skills at work again," Mortimer laughed. "So, this conference thingy, got room for one more?"

"We're making a lot of stops," Zeke warned as they made their way slowly across the room. "Daniel's not used to the bikes yet."

"Nothing wrong with taking things slow. Don't worry man, I won't cramp your style. I've just got this feeling, you know? Fate's hand at work? What were the odds we'd both stop for lunch at the same place at the same time, when I haven't seen you in two years?"

"We came across Daniel filling his face with blueberries in a random forest attached to a town you'd blink and miss. Ty liked the white picket fence at the B&B would you believe? It's the only reason we stopped." Zeke winked. "Trust in that feeling of yours. Maybe you'll get lucky."

"Ha!" Mortimer burst out laughing. "I get lucky all the time. Maybe this time I'll get super lucky."

/~/~/~/~/

"Four steak burgers, all rare, extra cheese and double eggs on two, One with pineapple and bacon, one with extra BBQ sauce and fries to the side." Ty handed back the menu to the cute waitress with a wink. "An extra bowl of fries would be welcome while we wait."

"Coming up." Switching her gum to the other side of her mouth, the waitress sashayed away.

Daniel didn't seem to notice. His head was jerking an inch to one side and then the other, and Ty noticed his eyes were darting everywhere. Laying his hand over Daniel's which was resting on the table, Ty felt the flinch he didn't see, but he didn't move his hand. "Babe, look at me." He had to repeat himself twice before Daniel heard and responded. His mate's sweet face was pale.

"Is there something specific that's bothering you? Did you want to switch chairs, is there something you need?"

"Nope." Daniel coughed and tried again. "No, it's all good thank you. Just, taking it all in. New place, you know?"

Ty didn't know. He was born a confident alpha bear shifter and had walked that walk his whole life. No place was too new, no situation too scary, and yet that is what Daniel smelled of - fear. Something that needed to be addressed if this trip had any chance of success.

"Babe, do you trust us – me and Zeke I mean?" Ty decided to attack the issue head on.

"Trust you?" A slight furrow appeared over Daniel's eyes. "I have very strong feelings for you – both of you. Is that what you mean? And is this really the place to talk about it?" His eyes started darting around the room again.

"It's the perfect place to talk about it. Daniel, look at me." Daniel's blue eyes met his. "That's right, now focus on me. No one else matters in this moment except you and I. Okay?"

Daniel gave a brief nod.

"Now, think about it. You're a writer. What does the word trust mean to you?"

Swallowing hard, Daniel said quietly, "it's a feeling of freedom, when you trust someone. Knowing that person always has your back no matter what, knowing that they put your needs first, that they don't lie, they don't cheat on you, they don't ever hurt you and that when you need them, they are there for you."

"Exactly," Ty smiled to show he was pleased. "You write characters who trust their mates all the time, with good reason, because no matter what you put those men through, their partners always have their back. Those characters are loved and cherished and they commit to their partners in every way – trust is the foundation for all of that."

"Those things are important to me," Daniel looked down to where their hands were still joined. "I poured my feelings and what I was hoping for in my own life, into my characters." He looked up. "But that's fiction, not the real world."

"Who says those fictional concepts can't be in the real world. When you've seen as much as I have over my life, hell, I see those concepts in action all the time. Wasn't it the philosopher Descartes who said if you can imagine it, then it's real?"

"Descartes is famous for saying, 'I think, therefore I am'." A small smile hovered around Daniel's lips. "The actual quote, or conclusion he came to if you like was, 'And as I observed that this truth, *I think, therefore I am*, was so certain and of such evidence that no ground of doubt, however extravagant, could be alleged by the Sceptics capable of shaking it, I concluded that I might, without scruple, accept it as the first principle of the philosophy of which I was in search'. My father loved to discuss philosophy."

"Ah," Ty was thrilled with his mate's amazing memory, and a little turned on by it. "But didn't Descartes conclude that those things he dreamed and those truths he found during the day were in fact the same thing? That they came from the same place?"

Daniel chuckled. "I can't believe we're debating philosophy in a truck stop. But yes, okay, if we accept that I know about the concepts I write about, whether imaginary, a dream, or from experience, and we hold that they are true concepts, then yes, it could be debated that those same concepts would be evident in the real world, for me to know about them in the first place."

"There you go. Point proved." Ty's smile widened. An animated Daniel was far prettier than a scared one. "My sweet cub, I know what we share together is all new to you, but one of the reasons Zeke used to insist I read to him from your books was because him and I could relate to every single one of your characters. Their bonds. The way they felt about each other is the way Zeke and I have felt for ten years. And now we feel the same way about you – don't you get it? You have those concepts you write about so well, in us and what we share together. Don't you see?"

The waitress chose that moment to deliver their fries. Ty could also see Morty and Zeke coming closer, so it was unlikely Daniel would answer. Ty just hoped his sweet mate would at least think about the things he said. *If our sweet cub could trust us, then ninety percent of his fears would just disappear, and he could enjoy himself.*

Chapter Thirteen

Daniel stepped out of the tiny shower and reached for his towel. The motel they'd stopped at for their first night away was clean and came with the right sized bed. But the bathroom facilities were tiny necessitating individual showers, much to Zeke's disgust. But Daniel welcomed the chance to decompress on his own. There was a lot to take in, his first day away from home, not least because it seemed Zeke's brother was coming along for the ride. Mortimer, "call me Morty", reminded him a lot of Zeke, not that Daniel said more than a dozen words to him so far, but the older bear carried the same easy confidence his mates had in spades.

More than I could ever have. Daniel eyed himself critically in the steamed over mirror. Ty's words about trust gave him a lot to think about on the afternoon ride, sitting behind Zeke, this time. It wasn't only Ty's words that haunted him, but the way he felt when he was looking into Ty's eyes. *Focus on me.* It was uncanny. Lost in Ty's gaze, it was as though the raucous sounds of the truckers, the calls of the waitresses, the piped music, even the smell of the cooking disappeared. All that mattered was the undivided attention of his mate.

I've not been fair to my mates. I've not been fair to my mates and that has to stop right now. That thought in mind, Daniel wrapped his towel around his hips, and went through to the bedroom. There was no sign of Morty. Zeke and Ty were dressed except for their boots, sprawled out on the bed, their arms around each other. "Ready for dinner?" Zeke rolled off the bed and reached for his boots. "Morty's gone ahead to reserve us a table. There's a local country and western band playing tonight which should be fun."

Straightening his shoulders, Daniel stood as tall as he was able to. "I haven't been fair to you as mates." There, he'd said it, but from the shocked looks on Zeke and Ty's faces, it wasn't enough. He was going to have to expand on his point. "Ty spoke to me about trust at lunchtime. I've been thinking about it."

"Babe, I didn't mean to upset you." Ty shuffled to the edge of the bed. "I was just trying to instill a bit of confidence in you, in us as a triad, that's all."

"No, no, you didn't upset me, but," Daniel licked his lips, his mouth dry, "I haven't trusted you as a mate should. I... my house... I just... my routine, my days, the things I did. I didn't change my life at all when you two came to live with me, and I should've done. You two gave up your traveling lifestyle without a second thought. I didn't realize how much I was trying to keep things the same, for me and my piece of mind. I owe you an apology. I'm sorry."

"Oh, my sweet cub." Before he could blink, Daniel was in his favorite place, surrounded by his mates. Strong arms held him as though he was special, his nose was filled with musk and the scents unique to the big bears who cared for him. And it was his favorite place, he realized. Not his office, not curled up in his big bed alone, but snuggled in his mates' arms.

"I'll do better, I promise," Daniel whispered, but his words were swallowed as his head was tilted back and Zeke took his lips with heat and passion. Ty was behind him, searing kisses across the nape of his neck, his hands tugging away Daniel's towel, curling around his butt cheeks.

His cock rose, pressing against Zeke's covered bulge and he tried to pull away, not wanting to make a mess of Zeke's jeans. But Ty's body wasn't letting him go anywhere, especially when Ty reached around him and grabbed Zeke's hips to anchor them all closer together. Much like their first night together, Daniel felt as though he was drowning, but this time he didn't shirk from doing some touching of his own. The three men rocked together, his mates' bulges teasing and tempting him, one against his cock, the other humping his ass crack.

His arms free, Daniel draped them over Zeke and Ty's shoulders, getting kissed by one and then the other. While kissing Ty, Zeke's beard dragged across his skin, eliciting all kinds of tingles as the man peppered his arched neck with nips and sucks strong enough to mark. When Zeke's lips were on his, Ty nuzzled his mating mark with teeth and tongue, every swipe designed to drive Daniel out of his mind. Zeke's closely shorn head was solid against his palm, while Ty's hair was silky to touch, sliding through his fingers. They were so different, and yet, they were both his. His mates.

It took Daniel a while to notice his hips were dancing all on their own, humping like a buck rabbit, stimulated as much by the sensual assault on his neck and lips as the pressure on his cock and butt. His skin was tight, his lungs were fit to burst. Orgasm was inevitable. His balls signaled the end was coming and there was nothing he could do to stop it, so he didn't try. Zeke's groan as the scent of his spunk hit the air sent his confidence into the stratosphere.

"Oh yeah." Ty stuttered and stilled behind him, leaning more heavily on Daniel this time. "Fuck, I need a clean pair of jeans, babe. These ones feel decidedly messy."

"Me too," Zeke huffed a laugh. "Thank the Fates for wet wipes. I'm not sure we'll get anymore hot water out of that shower. But first." Strong hands tilted Daniel's head up gently. "Cub, just be you, okay? You haven't let me or Ty down and while yes, we do want to take you out more, so we can show you off and create happy memories with you, that's a bear thing. Honestly, the moment you say you want to go home, then we will. No questions asked."

"But the conference, the people counting on me, your road trip, your brother..." Daniel was still rocking endorphins and wasn't sure he'd heard Zeke correctly.

"We needed to get you out of the house, little bear. You've created the perfect hideout. But for you to trust us completely, you need to see how committed we are to you outside the bedroom." Zeke glanced down at the wet spot on his jeans. "Perhaps not the best time to make a comment like that."

An unfamiliar feeling bubbled up inside of Daniel's gut and it took him a moment to identify it as joy. Laughing out loud, he tugged at Zeke's shirt that had come away from his jeans and swiped off the last of the spunk from his abs. "It seems your brother was right about one thing – I am the intelligent one. After all, I was the only one doing this naked." The slight tap on his ass from Zeke made him laugh even harder as Daniel went to find his clean clothes, leaving his menfolk to cope with the mess in their jeans.

Chapter Fourteen

Two hours into the evening, the bar was hopping, and Zeke was ever so slightly buzzed. The restaurant had just got in an order of fresh salmon which satisfied his bear and his hungry gut, and now, leaning back in his chair, he watched as more and more people made their way up to the dancefloor. The local band were well received and the mood in the room was lighthearted and fun. Zeke found his boot tapping the side of the table more than once.

Hmm, time to get up there and strut my stuff, he thought, eyeing his mates, trying to decide who he'd dance with first. Ty was relaxed and laughing over something Morty was saying. Ty never cared what anyone thought. If the locals didn't like two men dancing together, well that was just tough shit. There wasn't a law against it and besides throwing a few punches if anyone got rowdy about it, just made for good foreplay.

Daniel though... that was another matter. Zeke couldn't believe his sweet mate had spoken up the way he had back in their room. Those simple words; Daniel didn't realize it, but Zeke fell in love with his new mate in that moment. Those squared slender shoulders, the way Daniel tilted his chin, the firm voice stating what he saw as wrongdoings and a determination to make things right. It stirred an awareness in Zeke that his mate was not just a tag-along in their mating; he didn't just accept the way things were. Daniel thought about things, deeply.

Glancing down at Daniel sitting beside him, Zeke noticed the man was busy tapping something on his phone. Leaning slightly, because he wasn't going to intrude on Daniel's messages, he asked in a low voice, "are you busy telling your fans on social media you'll be at the conference?"

"What?" Daniel looked up surprised and his cheeks bloomed bright red. "Er… not exactly." He held up his phone, and Zeke squinted in the half light, getting his eyes to adjust to the bright screen.

Light catching the planes of his face, the hat sending half in shadow.

Her easy smile – skirt and hair flowing in time to the music.

Drummer hunched, hidden by his instruments, rising up to punctuate the song.

Lowered eyes, sideways glances, the slight upturn of the lips…

"I've never been in any kind of club before," Daniel said shyly, snapping off his phone and putting it in his pocket. "You can get so much more from an experience when you're actually in it, or so I've found this evening. I'm making notes for my stories – impressions from watching people having fun."

"I can make this evening more memorable for you," Zeke waggled his eyebrows that made his beard twitch.

Daniel laughed. "I think you did that before we came out for dinner."

Putting down his beer can, Zeke held out his hand. "I'd love it if you would dance with me. It's just a basic two-step, I'm sure you'll pick it up, if you haven't done it before."

He could see it, the moment Daniel's fears and desire to remain hidden resurfaced. But ignoring everything and everyone else, he kept his gaze on his mate's face. *Trust us. Trust me.* Zeke was just about to drop his hand, when Daniel slipped his on top of it. "I'll have you know the only thing I've ever danced with is a broom in the privacy of my own living room. If I tread all over your feet, don't start crying at me."

"I'm sure my size fourteens can cope." Standing, Zeke gently tugged

Daniel with him. "Just follow my lead."

/~/~/~/~/

"Oh, our sweet cub, he's come so far in such a short time." Ty couldn't stop his grin if he tried. Just like in the truck stop, Daniel was keeping his eyes on Zeke constantly, and Zeke was just as attentive, holding their mate close, moving so as not to allow anyone to come into contact with Daniel. It was like watching a love story unfold, and Ty beamed. They looked beautiful together – Zeke's ruggedness a perfect foil for Daniel's ethereal beauty.

"That joy of yours might be short lived." Nudging Ty's arm, Mortimer directed his attention to a table off to the side. The four guys there couldn't stop watching Zeke and Daniel, in between snarling among themselves. Their anger was palpable across the room, and Ty's fingers curled into a fist.

"I will not let Zeke and Daniel's first dance be spoiled by a bunch of guys threatened by something beautiful. You with me, Morty?"

"Hell, yeah." Morty stood and pumped his biceps. "Let's quietly dissuade them from causing any trouble, shall we?"

"Quietly, loudly. I don't give a fuck, so long as the band keeps playing and my mates keep dancing." Stepping around the table, Ty headed across the room, trusting Morty was right behind him. Standing so they were blocking the men's view of the dance floor, Ty folded his arms across his chest. "Do you guys have a problem with people having an enjoyable time."

"Fuck yeah. You're with them, ain't yah? Are you all taking it up the ass? Fucking faggots." A dirty blond guy who needed a shower and a shave sneered.

"Your ignorance is showing," Ty snarled. "Did you know, the original meaning of the word faggots referred to a bundle of sticks folks used to bundle together to burn for fuel. I'm not seeing anyone setting a fire on the dance floor, are you Morty?"

"All I'm seeing is good folks having a pleasant evening. We aim to make sure it stays that way." Morty slapped one fist into his open palm. "Shall we take this outside?"

"Like fuck," the blond blustered, the size of Morty's biceps finally piercing his drunken haze. "I'm not going outside with you. You just want to push me down and shove your cock in my face. That's all you gays ever do."

"I wouldn't let you near my cock without a tetanus shot." Morty grinned, "but fine, have it your way. Throw the first punch, *chickenshit.*"

That was all it took. Chairs tipped over as the men stumbled to their feet. The blond aimed a sloppy punch at Morty's gut and the fight was on.

/~/~/~/~/

Hearing the commotion, Daniel broke Zeke's gaze and glanced to the side. "Oh, no, Ty!"

"No, no, no, little cub." Zeke's finger tilted Daniel's chin back to him. "He and Morty are just having a bit of fun. The band's still playing, and I want your focus on me."

"He could get hurt." Daniel tried to peer around the other side of Zeke, but the infuriating man executed a quick turn and all Daniel could see was the band and Zeke was right, they were still playing. The drummer flicked a quick look in the direction of the fight, and when a table crashed, he just hit his skins with a bit more force and the singer increased his volume. A few people left the dance floor, the men rolling up their sleeves, the women running to the bar, but the band didn't stop, and Zeke kept dancing.

"Z, please. Aren't you worried about our mate?"

"If I was worried, I would have stashed you behind the bar and gone to help," Zeke whispered against his ear. "But it's Ty and Morty against a half a dozen humans at most. Just keep dancing."

"Is this one of those trust lessons?" Daniel still couldn't see what was going on. He could hear enough. Shouts, yells, the sound of flesh on flesh, glasses breaking and the occasional cheer. He winced at what sounded like a window smashing almost drowning out the band.

"You are so damn clever," Zeke grinned, his big hand warm on Daniel's jaw. Even with the ruckus around them, Zeke remained like an immovable mountain. "Ty and Morty are fighting to keep us safe. Ty can focus because he knows I'm with you.

I can focus on you, because I trust my brother to watch Ty's back and Ty's a powerhouse in his own right. All you have to do is listen to the music, focus on me, and move that sexy body of yours."

"If Ty has one bruise on him, one teeny tiny scratch, you're both going to see how I get when I'm angry." Daniel warned.

"And that's why I love you," Zeke said easily, swinging him around in time to the music. "Because your anger shows how much you care. Now, dance babe. Ty and Morty are seeing to it we'll not be interrupted, and this could be our song, don't you think?"

Swaying softly to the strains of *Forever and Ever, Amen*, Daniel did his best to ignore the sounds of the fight and focused on his first ever dance with his mate. *And did I hear right? Did Zeke just tell me he loves me? Oh... My... Gods!*

Chapter Fifteen

"You got kicked out of the bar! And look at the state of your clothes! Ty Hollifield, I should kick your ass for you. Just look at this cut above your eye. What if it becomes infected?"

Zeke passed Morty a wash cloth, sharing a grin with his brother. They were in Morty's room, having left as soon as the police turned up at the bar to break up the fight. As Daniel warned, he was a spitfire when he was angry, and it was a wonder he managed to keep his rant under wraps until they got back to the motel room.

"And fighting? What is it about you big lugs and fighting? This was our first date as a triad and you started throwing your fists around. Is this what it's going to be like every time we go anywhere?" Zeke noticed, despite the tirade, Daniel was washing Ty's face gently. Ty smirked in Zeke's direction which was a dumb move especially when Daniel saw it.

"Oh, so you think this is funny, do you?" Daniel actually stomped his foot and Zeke had to put his hand over his mouth. "Fighting is not funny. Civilized people do not throw others out of a huge window and laugh about it."

"Oh my god, you should have seen that idiot's face though," Morty slapped his knee, chuckling loudly. "Ty had him in a headlock and lifted him straight off the floor and just threw him. It was..."

"Do not complete that sentence," Daniel gave a cute little snarl, topping it off by throwing the wash cloth he was using on Ty at Morty's face. "You're just as bad. Sitting there with your chin all black and blue and thinking it's funny. You guys have got rocks in your head, that's what you've got. Solid rocks. If this is an example of bear mating habits, then it's no wonder I prefer staying at home."

"Aww, babe," Ty tried his puppy dog expression. It was a powerful tool, those big eyes and down turned mouth. Zeke had fallen for it a hundred times, powerless to resist. "Those guys will think twice about picking on a gay couple again. They didn't think they'd get their asses kicked. Morty and I were doing a public service, babe."

"Do not try your puppy dog look on me, Ty Hollifield. It won't work."

This is priceless. Zeke couldn't help himself, the laughter just bubbled out of him, and he bent over, cackling like a mad man. Morty didn't help, he was just as bad, and then Ty started sniggering and that was the final straw for Daniel.

"You guys are a clan of boneheads," Daniel glared. "You're all as bad as each other. Well, fine, if you all think this is funny, you can all bunk in together. I'm going to our room and I'm locking the door. Good night." Striding across the small room, he pulled open the door, stepping through, before slamming it behind him.

There was a moment's silence and then Zeke made the mistake of catching Ty's eye and they were both laughing their fool heads off again. Morty couldn't stop chuckling although he was saying "shush, shush," and pointing to the adjoining wall. Daniel would hear them, of course he would with shifter hearing, but Zeke couldn't help himself.

"Guess we're sleeping on the floor, big guy," Ty wheezed as he tried to pull himself together. "I doubt that fiery cub of ours will be unlocking the door before morning."

"Well, you ain't kicking me out of my bed," Morty grumbled, snagging the covers and rolling them over his shoulder. "There'll be extra blankets and pillows in the cupboard. You can bunk down anywhere that's not with me."

"Are you okay?" Zeke leaned over, licking across the cut on the top of Ty's eye. It was already healing.

"I'm fine," Ty said, still chuckling softly as he rested his head on Zeke's shoulder. "I'd do it all over again, just for the chance of seeing you and our cub dancing. You looked beautiful together."

"Maybe next time, we'll go to a gay-friendly place, and then all of us can dance together." Wrapping his arm around Ty's shoulder, Zeke ran his free hand down Ty's tight torso to the lump in his pants. "I don't suppose you fancy a blow job in the bathroom? We might just both fit."

"That wouldn't be fair on Daniel, he'd be able to hear us," Ty said ruefully, moving Zeke's hand away. "He did have a right to be mad. Technically, it was our first date as a threesome. Not the best impression to make."

"I think you'll be surprised," Zeke said. "We're trying to encourage him to trust us. Hopefully, tonight's brawl will show him we can keep him safe, no matter what. He's quite a thinker, is our mate."

"And at the moment, he's probably regretting locking the door on us, but you're right, his pride will stop him opening it until morning. But I don't want him feeling excluded, if he hears us having sexy times without him. He'd think we didn't care if he was with us or not."

"You're right as always," Zeke brushed a kiss across Ty's temple. "So, tell me, what started the fight anyway." Zeke knew neither he nor Ty would get much sleep while Daniel was in another room. But that was okay. They'd keep their mate safe, even if he wasn't aware of it.

/~/~/~/~/

"There you go again. You and your big mouth and now you're stuck sleeping by yourself, all because you let your temper get away from you."

Daniel kept his voice to a mumble, thumping his pillow into submission. He could not get comfortable. Five years he'd slept in his custom-sized bed by himself. Just over a week with his mates, and the similar sized bed he was in now felt cold and lonely. Daniel didn't think he'd feel any better if he was at home. Zeke and Ty were like a furnace around him at night, and the room seemed too quiet without their melodic snores.

Truth be told, Ty's fighting was frightening to him. Daniel was still dancing with Zeke when the police burst in. There was a lot of yelling and orders to "stand down" and while Ty and Morty had been exonerated – apparently the other party had thrown the first punch, Daniel still didn't see why the fight was necessary in the first place.

Protecting him. That's what Zeke had said, but Daniel had to wonder if it'd been better to have received a hiding himself, than be confronted with the sight of blood pouring down the side of Ty's handsome face. The man had a grin from ear to ear, and waffled something about how head wounds always looked worse than they were. But that wasn't just a tiny scratch – it was a cut. One of the guys he was fighting had a knife. Ty took out a man with a knife, with his bare hands. His bare hands, not his bear hands, his bare freaking hands.

Daniel shivered, wrapping his blanket tighter around his shoulders, but he couldn't get warm. The only people he had to talk to about any of this were his mates – *and I locked them out,* he thought sadly, looking across at the door. *They'd want to be with me, right?*

Determined not to second guess himself, Daniel crept out of bed and turned the lock on the door. Now, when Ty and Zeke wanted to sneak into their room, they could, and Daniel would wake up all warm and toasty, probably with a cock nudging his lips. His favorite way to wake up. Snuggling under the blankets again, he closed his eyes, dreaming of a blow job triangle, with Ty and Zeke trying to hold out, not wanting to come first. *They are so competitive,* he thought with a smile.

/~/~/~/~/

Ty's bear woke him up with a prod and a growl. He listened, but whatever the danger was, it wasn't in their room. Morty and Zeke were conducting a snoring duet, the parking lot outside was quiet. Straining hard, Ty could just make out the sound of a door handle turning, and he frowned. It wasn't the door to their room; he and Zeke were curled up in front of it. A faint squeal of a hinge let him know the door was opened successfully. *Fucking hell, it's Daniel's door.*

"Wake up," he hissed furiously, shaking Zeke's shoulder. "Someone's trying to get into the cub's room."

"Daniel locked the door, no one can get in," Zeke said sleepily. He was never alert when he first woke up.

"He must have unlocked it, thinking we'd try and sneak in. But now some other bastard's in there."

That woke Zeke up. "I'll kill any fucking bastard who…." A yell of fright, a loud series of thumps. Ty and Zeke were on their feet in seconds, slamming open the door to Morty's room and running the ten feet to Daniel's door, the concrete cold under their bare toes. The door was open, and Ty was greeted with a sight he prayed he never saw again as long as they lived.

Daniel had clearly been sleeping, his hair mussed, his naked body struggling between two of the thugs Ty'd taken out earlier that night. As he ran into the room and flicked on the light, Ty wasn't quick enough to stop a punch from a third man that knocked Daniel's head back with a crack. Zeke growled.

"Close the door, Ty. We've got dead men walking."

"My brother's in jail because of you, asshole." Ty could see the family resemblance, but it didn't make any difference. His bear surged forward, and he could feel his claws spring from his fingertips and hair emerge up his arms.

"Your brother came at me with a fucking knife," Ty lifted the corner of his lip, showing his elongated fangs. The man's face went white. "You could have left well enough alone. You could've just taken your hiding like a man and let us ride through. But no, you kept on drinking, even after the cops told you to go home and sleep it off, and now you've attacked our reason for living. What makes you think you're getting out of this room alive?"

"Hey, cuz, we didn't sign up for any of this freaky shit." The men holding Daniel let him go and he slumped to the floor.

"I don't know what the hell you two are, but we're out of here," the other one said.

"You're not going anywhere," Zeke promised, his fangs gleaming under the light. "You broke into the room of an unarmed man...."

"The door was unlocked," one of the men protested.

"And now it's locked." Shifting his hand completely into a paw, Ty curled it around the door lock and squeezed. The metal gave way under his paw with a scrunch. "Got anything else to say with your last breaths?"

"Fuck, I'm never drinking again," The one who claimed brother status to the jailed man shook wildly, backing up towards the window. Out of the corner of his eye, Ty saw Zeke had shifted completely and was standing over Daniel's limp body, snarling at the two men he had pinned by the bed. "Look, I don't care if you're poo pushers, I don't care what you fucking do. Just let us get out of here, and I'll swear on a stack of bibles I'll never come near your kind again."

"And what kind would that be?" Ty asked sauntering slowly towards the man who was frantically trying to get the window open. "The gay kind, or the kind of man who can change into a hairy-assed bear."

"Either, neither, I don't care. I'm not gonna mess with anybody. Let me out of here," the man screamed as Ty shifted, his clothes shredding as his bear took over. In the shifter world, justice was swift and messy. Daniel was crumpled like a discarded rag on the floor. Ty's bear was incensed. Nothing was going to make him feel better until the perpetrators' blood was spilled.

Ty couldn't stand up on his hind legs in bear form, the ceiling was too low. But he spread his front feet wide, rolling his massive shoulders, his eyes fixed on his prey. The sudden stench of urine was an annoyance, but Ty ignored it. He wasn't going to be satisfied until he smelled blood. Squeezing his bulk past the bed, he lifted his lips, showing off his pearly white, and very sharp teeth. The man was babbling, curled up in a heap, making his bargains with a God he clearly didn't believe in considering all the hate he carried in his heart. Raising his paw, Ty took a moment to flex his claws, just because he could. The man was as good as dead.

And that's when Ty heard it, the sweet sound of his cub's voice. Tired, pain laced in every word. "Please, don't kill them." *Well, fuck it.* Ty dropped his paw and snarled.

Chapter Sixteen

His head pounding, his cheek and jaw throbbing, it took a moment for Daniel to get a handle on why Zeke was standing over him growling like a freight train, and why both of his mates were in their shifted forms. Tilting his head slightly, he could just see Ty advancing near the window, the stench of the man's fear was strong. "Please, don't kill them." Daniel winced when Ty snarled.

Zeke dropped his head, his long snout sniffing over Daniel's hair and unbruised cheek. "I'm fine," Daniel said quietly, reaching up and touching the puffy side of his face gingerly. "It's fine, honestly. I just need to get up. Please."

Shuffling to one side, Zeke stayed close as Daniel sluggishly got to his feet, grateful for his mate's thick legs and broad shoulders. Using Zeke's body to lean on, because his head was still swimming, Daniel took the blanket Zeke swiped for him with his claws and then took in the scene. The two men staring at him in shock trapped by the bed, the third intruder a mumbling mess on the floor by the window, still loomed over by Ty.

"Well this is a fine fucking mess," Daniel shook his head and then wished he hadn't. It was at times like this the mind link would come in handy, although the stances of his bear mates were easy to read. He caught the eye of one of the two men Zeke was keeping contained. "What the fuck were you thinking, breaking in and attacking me for no reason?"

"It was Bob's idea," the man flicked his head in the direction of the window. "His poppa's going to be right pissed to hear John's in jail again. And he's been banned for life from his momma's favorite restaurant because this is the third time he's been kicked out of there. She ain't going to be happy about that the next time she wants to have her birthday celebrations there and we can't go."

"Then you should've thought of that before you acted like jerks. Why on earth did the idea of me and Zeke dancing together get you so damn angry? I assume that's why the fight in the restaurant started."

"Didn't bother me much." The chatty man nudged his friend with his elbow. "Did it bother you?"

"It bothered John," the other man grimaced. "Probably made him hot in his britches if truth be known. He's always scared shitless someone will notice how he keeps eying up men's dicks in the locker room. You ask me, Bob ain't much better. Not that there's anything wrong with that," he added quickly as Zeke growled.

"There's an enormous difference between being a pervert and being gay," Daniel said angrily. "Contrary to ignorant belief, gay guys aren't that desperate for cock they molest anyone they see, gay or straight, just so they can get off. Gay men have as much right to find love and form relationships just the same as straight men do. There's no difference except in the people they're attracted to. Zeke and I dancing didn't hurt anyone else. It wasn't your toes I was standing on."

Zeke chuffed softly as though he was laughing, and Daniel threaded his fingers through the long hair on his mate's shoulder. "We've got one hell of a mess here, guys," he said quietly. "I'm not sensing a lot of intelligence in the room, but all three of these bozos have seen you shift. Combine that with alcohol and blabber mouths and we could have a situation." He sighed. "I'm sorry I stopped you killing them. Maybe if I left the room...."

"No, don't do that. Don't go," one of the cousins yelled quickly, grabbing onto his brother's arm. "Honestly, we didn't see nothing. Nothing at all. Too drunk to remember anything. Fuck, for all I know I'm still in bed. That's it. That's what this is, it's a dream, a damn freaky one, but a dream nonetheless and in this dream, I'm gonna to sleep walk my ass right out of this room just as soon as your big assed bear lets me get near the door, and I ain't ever coming back."

"What do you think, guys?" Daniel looked over to see Ty sitting down, his nose tilted away from Bob, probably because urine wasn't the only thing Daniel could smell. Damn, that guy was a mess. Zeke nudged him carefully, his snout fur tickling over the swelling in his cheek. Daniel immediately understood. "I know they hurt me, but I'll be fine after some sleep. Come on, let them go. If they tell anyone what they saw, well who are they going to tell? They broke into this room and attacked an unarmed man which is illegal no matter which state you're in. And then they start spouting off about how the man they were attacking was defended by other men who can turn into bears? No one will believe them and from the sounds of things, they're known drunks and trouble makers."

"The worst," one of the cousins assured him, nodding his head. "The cops don't listen to a word we say, mostly cos we're always drunk. And besides, you guys aren't staying long are you?"

"We're leaving in the morning." Daniel thought things through quickly. Zeke paid for their motel rooms, using a credit card listed to his business, whatever that was. Daniel paid for the dinner and drinks, also with a credit card, but the only address on that was a P.O. box he used for author related correspondence. No one knew where he lived, and it wasn't likely that anything could be tracked from Zeke to their home address. His mates had been alive too long to not let that happen. And besides, if they did get tracked down, there was nothing anyone could find. It's not as though he had a shifter bear clan sign on his front gate.

"Shall we take a vote?" Daniel asked his bears. The humans' votes wouldn't count – it wasn't their survival on the line. "All in favor of letting them go?" Daniel raised his hand. Zeke snarled for a moment but raised his paw slowly. "Come on, babe," Daniel said to Ty. "I know they hurt me, but you don't want to eat them now. That guy smells like he's shit his pants. That's just nasty."

Ty raised his paw and Daniel was just about to call that a win, when the paw landed over Ty's nose as he showed his teeth. "You can't block your nose and kill someone at the same time," Daniel laughed, despite the ache in his jaw. "Let's get them out of here before they stink up the room permanently."

"Those bears understand what you're saying?" One of the cousins asked, his eyes wide.

"They understand me. They don't understand people like you at all, beating up on others just because of who they love. I suggest you get out of here before they decide not to listen to me either. And take that stinky cousin with you."

Daniel didn't have to say it twice. The cousins grumbled a bit, dragging their mumbling kin with them, but they made it to the door. "Er... sir?" One of the cousins said cautiously, "one of your bears mangled the door lock. We can't get out."

"For the love of...." Striding over to the window, his blanket flapping around his ankles, Daniel managed to get the locks open and slid it up as far as it would go. "Climb out there and fucking think twice before you go breaking into a room again."

The two cousins looked as though they might argue, but a snarl from Ty who was still lurking by the window moved them quick enough. Within a few minutes the intruders were gone.

Daniel thought about closing the window, but the lingering smell of Bob's crap changed his mind. Sitting on the corner of the bed, Daniel touched his cheek again – it was still sore, although not as bad as when he was hit. He looked up to see Zeke and Ty watching him closely, still in fur. "Do you guys have a problem with us waking Morty and leaving early, maybe catching some breakfast later down the road? I know it ruins our itinerary, but I'm not sure I'm going to get any sleep here with what's left of the night, morning, whatever."

Ty shifted first. "You should've let me kill him," he said, anger still lacing his tone as he gently stroked Daniel's cheek. Leaning into the touch, Daniel sighed as Zeke came up on the other side of him, enclosing them all in his huge arms.

"Killing them would be so messy," Daniel placed his hand over Zeke's heart, the steady thump comforting him more than anything else. "There's the blood to get out of the carpet, and probably the bedding too. Then there's bodies to dispose of, graves to dig – it's not as though there's a 24/7 store handy that would sell us a shovel. I'd far rather we just got on the road and got out of here. After you've fixed the lock, Ty."

"The lock's a goner, besides Zeke paid for the room, he can cover the cost of a new door too," Ty managed a chuckle. "No mate of mine is climbing out of a window." Then he let out a huff and Daniel tried not to be distracted by so much nakedness. He was still only wearing a blanket, and his mates' clothes were only fit for the rubbish bin. "Babe," Ty was serious now, "why did you leave your door unlocked? I thought you said you were locking us out for the night."

"That does not make what happened my fault. You were the one who started all this by having Bob's cousin put in jail because of fighting," Daniel glared. "I did lock the door. Then I unlocked the door because silly me thought my mates couldn't bear to be apart from me and having them hanging around the door would be embarrassing. Is it my fault if my two mates fell asleep before they came knocking to see if they could get in? Hmm? Hmm? Yeah, just as I thought," he added when he was greeted with two pairs of red cheeks. "It would be kinda nice if you two made a bit more of an effort next time. No mated cub should sleep alone, EVER."

"And you never will again," both men promised him.

Chapter Seventeen

Their second day and night on the road proved uneventful, but Zeke felt a prickle of awareness crawling up his neck as they rode into Roswell around midday of the third day. The writer's convention was being held in a hall on the outskirts of town, but the hotel the four of them would be staying at was within walking distance of all the major attractions – the UFO museum, the art gallery and the numerous shops dedicated to arts, crafts and all things alien. It was a surprisingly large town. Zeke hadn't been there since before the alien incident. But then his uneasiness could have had something to do with the officious looking young man who greeted them, clipboard in hand, in the foyer of the hotel.

"You're with the convention, right? Only if you aren't, I'm sorry we're all booked out here. Only MM authors, support staff, and of course our lovely readers will be staying here over the next five days. You don't look like you're in the convention." He gave Ty the once over, from head to toe and back again. "Of course, you could be entertainment. I'm not sure exactly what they've got planned this year, but if you are entertaining us, well, let me be the first to greet *you*, sugar plum."

There was something false about the cocky man's attitude, and Zeke couldn't put his finger on what it was, but his blatant flirting with Ty was enough to piss Zeke off. "Excuse me, we don't want to be taking up more of your time than necessary," he said, adding emphasis to the last part. "Is the author D.B. Bear on your list of approved persons?"

"Well, of course," the man didn't even need to check his clipboard. "It's a huge honor they're going to be speaking at the convention this year. They've never been seen at an event like this before and they have thousands of loyal fans who can't wait to meet them. But I'm afraid you'll have to wait until Thursday before they're available."

"Is there any reason you're using they and their pronouns for a male author?" Morty growled.

For the first time, the man looked flustered, but he recovered quickly. "I'm being respectful," he said hotly. "A lot of writers in the MM field are women, but they use initials or non-gender specific author names for reasons of anonymity. We also have trans authors and others who identify along various points of the gender spectrum. I'm not going to assume a famed author's gender, orientation, or pronouns until I meet them personally and ask them."

"I'm sure the authors and their supporters appreciate your sensitivity." He still didn't ring true to Zeke, but the bear could be polite when he had to. "Now could you please direct us to D.B. Bear's suite.

We've been on the road for two days...."

"I told you, I'm sorry," the man interrupted rudely. "We never give out room details about any of our guests at the conference. They won't be available until Thursday. Of course, they're supposed to be checking in today, so you might see them around tomorrow, but...."

"That is what we're trying to do, man. Check in," Zeke fumed, tugging a reluctant Daniel forward. "*This* is D.B. Bear. Now can we get the key to our suite, please?"

"You're D.B. Bear?" The man looked Daniel up and down, but this time there was no flirting edge to his inspection. If anything, he'd looked Daniel over and found him lacking which made Zeke seethe all the more. "But... you can't be. I've spoken to you online a hundred times. You must remember me? Saul? I've read all your books over and over and they are full of sensitivity and passion. I could have sworn...."

"That I'd be a woman?" Daniel sighed. "Nice to meet you in the flesh Saul. I identify as a gay male. My preferred pronouns are he and him. Are you going to allow us to our suite or not? As you pointed out, this is my first trip to an event like this one. I'm hot, tired, and covered in dust. If you don't believe who I am then fine. You can explain to Pat, Stormy, and any fan who wants to meet me, that I won't be here. Gentlemen, it's time to find another hotel."

"No, wait," Saul cried as Daniel turned to leave. "I'm sorry. I truly am. It's just, I... never mind." Clutching his clipboard, he said in a firmer tone. "You have the executive suite on the top floor. We only had a booking for you and two guests, however, the suite contains three bedrooms and I am sure two of your... entourage can double up." The pause was barely there, but Zeke heard it. The man was fishing for information.

"Thank you. I'm sure there'll be plenty of room," Zeke said firmly. "If you'll excuse us." Dropping his voice so only shifters could hear, he muttered, "Let's get the hell out of here."

/~/~/~/~/

"What the hell was that asshole's problem," Ty angrily stabbed the elevator button for the top floor. "He looked positively shocked to see you were a man. Who the hell cares what gender a person is if they like their work?"

"It's an issue in the romance genre. In the whole literary world actually," Daniel said tiredly. "Some people don't like it that it's mostly women who write romance. Some men complain that they don't get a fair showing in MM because there are so many women writing it. Some women use initials or even male pen names to publish their books in the MM genre. Some men use women's names when they write MF stories. Some people are honest about it, but there has been the odd author who has built up whole new persona on social media that is basically founded on lies. Then, because of the internet, readers find out, the person is exposed, and readers and other authors feel betrayed because they've been lied to. It's why I don't share a lot about myself on social media, for that reason."

"That could probably be misconstrued as well," Ty grumbled. The elevator stopped, and the doors opened out directly into a lovely suite "Thank goodness he gave us a key to stop people coming up here whenever they like." Ty waited until they'd all exited the elevator and then sent it back down, locking the door to their suite so it wouldn't automatically open if the elevator came back up. "Honestly, babe, what do you think about all this? Do you care, when you read someone else's books, what gender they are? I know I don't, and I read a lot."

"Of course, I don't." Shrugging off his jacket, Daniel threw it on the chair. "I look for strong characters, a good plot and an easy to read writing style. The politics of this business is not something I get involved in. I know I would be hated for saying something like that publicly, but I am who I am. A bear shifting omega who happens to write MM and MMM romance stories, because I'm gay and like to dream about men. I put my stories out for sale and if I'm lucky, my readers like the sample well enough to buy it. That's it, as far as I'm concerned. There are a lot of wonderfully talented authors in the romance genre, contemporary and paranormal, men and women. I don't care what they have between their legs, or who they sleep with at night. And while I'm here, I should probably keep that to myself too."

For the first time since he suggested coming, Ty wondered if they were right to force Daniel to be at this conference. But Daniel hadn't finished. "I mean, if you look at things logically, my social media profile is a lie too. I don't tell anyone I'm a bear shifter, for obvious reasons. But I write about shifters, not only bears admittedly, but shifters and the paranormal world in general. My readers assume I've made up the rules of my worlds, even though to me they're factual and based on the teachings my father gave me. But what am I to do? Tell everyone when I give my speech on Friday, that I am a bear shifter and in the interests of transparency I decided to out myself and the whole paranormal world?"

The three older bears looked at each other in alarm. "Daniel, you're tired and out of your comfort zone, which is making you stressed," Morty said gently. "You know our reasons for secrecy the same as the rest of us here."

"But what makes my secret any different to the ones about gender or sexuality that a random few authors hide?" Daniel cried. "Do you hear me slagging off other authors because they write about sexual activities they could never experience because of their bits or lack of them? No. I don't use my biography to raise money, con people, or anything illegal like that. But my secret is no worse or better than say a female author pretending to be male, or a male pretending to be female, or someone pretending to be trans when they're not, or someone who is trans who hides it. They're still secrets and while we have perfectly good reasons for keeping ours, those people who have secrets think the same way. How is that any different?"

"Babe, the shifter council would send enforcers after us, if you breathed a word of what we are to non-shifters."

Ty was worried. Daniel was working himself up into distraught territory.

"But we did exactly that just the other night." Tears were falling down Daniel's cheeks and Ty crossed the room to hug him, but Daniel moved out of his reach. "You two shifted in front of humans. Yes, you were going to kill them, and you were protecting me, but because of me you let them go and they might tell someone who does believe them. And now I'm here at a conference, ready to spread more lies about who I am, and who you are to me. We pride ourselves as shifters for not lying, because it can be scented by others of our kind, but we lie all the fucking time."

"We have to hide our bears," Daniel had worked up to a full blown rant now. "We have to hide our relationship with each other because we're a triad and society frowns on that – worse because we're three men. I have some snot nosed person downstairs judging me because I didn't look like the person he imagined I'd be. But that's exactly it. I consider myself a person. I write as D. B. Bear. That's it. That's all I know. And I can't be honest with anyone outside of this room and it's tearing me up inside. It's why I hide. I don't know how to be what's expected of me. I mean, fuck, I meet the first person at this conference, who I have had conversations with online and for all the chats we've shared, he hates me just from looking at me."

Ty's heart ached, feeling Daniel's pain as if it were his own. A quick glance at Zeke showed the same pain on his face. "I'll take the end room," Morty said quietly, shouldering his bag and disappearing, understanding their need for privacy.

"I'm sorry," Daniel sobbed. "I'm so very sorry. I don't mean to be a burden, but I just don't get how to do this."

Ty wasn't sure what the 'this' was, but neither he nor his bear could stand seeing their mate so upset. He moved closer, hovering, but not wanting to be rejected again. "Babe, we'll go home, now," he said, looking over at Zeke who nodded quickly. "It's me who's sorry. I thought this trip would be good for you, but clearly, it's too much too soon. We, me and Zeke, we didn't understand the issues you're going through, and I've got to be honest, I'm not sure I do now. But it hurts me to see you like this. Whatever you want, we'll do it, right now. Anything to see you smile again."

"Just hold me, please?" Daniel held out both hands and Ty only just beat Zeke getting to him. Zeke, always the man of few words, wrapped his arms around them both lending them his strength, while Ty dried Daniel's tears with his fingers. "You must think I'm an emotional mess," Daniel said a long minute later, his head on Ty's chest, his fingers curled in Zeke's shirt above his heart. "I want to be with you both. I want to be able to walk out of here, holding your hands, staking my claim so shits like that fucking Saul downstairs don't think they can flirt with you."

"Saul pissed me off too," Zeke grumbled. "I'm sure you could tell."

"If you want to let people know we're together, then do it," Ty said gently.

"But you said it would be better if people thought you were my bodyguards."

Ty shrugged and caught Zeke's eye. "I've been known to make mistakes. Not many," he added as Zeke chuckled. "I'm not ashamed to lay claim to both of you in public – to hell with what anyone thinks."

Zeke added, "I feel the same way."

"So, if you're happy to introduce us as your partners, then that's what we'll do," Ty continued. "If you want to skip the conference, then we'll just be a public threesome everywhere else. Babe, it's up to you. We just want you to feel comfortable outside our home."

"That might take a little while." Daniel took a shaky breath, and then another. "I need to ask one more question."

"Anything," Ty said, while Zeke nodded.

"Well, it's more than one, actually, but they're all related. The other night," Daniel tilted his head, so he could see Zeke's face, "you told me you loved me on the dance floor – or words to that effect. Did you mean that? And if you did, why haven't you said it again? And you Ty," he shifted his head, so he could look at Ty directly, "do you feel that way too? And if so, why haven't you said anything?"

"I should've known, jammy Z would get in first," Ty chuckled. "We were supposed to be doing a romantic setting for professions of love, just like in your stories. You're an asshole Z, jumping the gun like that."

"It was a romantic scene," Zeke smirked. "The music was playing, our mate was fighting for our right to dance together, it was the perfect setting. And yes, little cub," he said cupping Daniel's jaw, "I meant it then and I mean it now. Ty will tell you I'm not one for mushy stuff, but never doubt you and Ty hold an equal place in my heart, even if you don't hear the words that often, okay?"

Daniel's bottom lip trembled as his eyes lit up. "As for me," Ty said, reclaiming Daniel's attention, "I loved you from when I saw you with your fur full of blueberry juices. I knew from that instant you were the one who would make us complete. The only reason I didn't say anything was because Z and I agreed we'd take you out for a romantic dinner, or do something special for the big love reveal."

"The big love reveal," Daniel grinned. "I'll have to remember that for one of my stories." He took in a huge breath. "I'm so glad you guys feel this way. I didn't want the love to be one-sided in our mating."

"You love us too?" Ty's previously aching heart bounced with happiness. "I know you're shy, but it's easy to say the words. I. Love. You. Ty." He enunciated in an exaggerated fashion.

"Or, you could say. I. Love. You. Zeke." Zeke stuck his tongue out at Ty.

"Hmm," Daniel tapped his bottom lip with his finger. "What if I said, I. Love. You. My Alphas."

"That's perfect." Ty made sure he got to claim the first kiss with their sweet cub. Not that Zeke seemed to mind. He just pushed his bearded lips in the smush so they were all connected, the way they should be.

Chapter Eighteen

I can do this, I can do this, I can do this. Daniel had dressed with care. His freshly pressed pants showed his ass off to perfection – he'd checked in the mirror even after Zeke and Ty told him he looked amazing. His blue button up shirt was left open at the collar, but matched his eyes perfectly. He braided the side pieces of his hair, and attached the braids at the back of his head to stop it falling in his face. Daniel wasn't hiding anymore. He was stepping out with his men… and Morty who said he was hungry, but Daniel knew he was being supportive, which was sweet.

It was just dinner in the hotel. The conference didn't start properly until the next morning. Daniel had checked his phone before stepping into the elevator and knew that his two main online friends, Pat and Stormy had checked in, and they'd made arrangements to meet up the next day. The name tags wouldn't go on until the conference started, so tonight he could enjoy the anonymity with his mates. His wonderfully sweet and understanding mates.

As the elevator shuddered to a stop on the ground floor, Zeke and Ty offered their arms. One breath in, one breath out, Daniel slipped his hands into the offered elbows as the door opened. The foyer was busier than when they'd arrived. The reception desk was crowded, and clumps of people stood around, peering at every new arrival.

Readers, writers, it was hard to tell who was who. It wasn't as though writers had gold stars on their head, or shiny fingers or anything that made them stand out from a crowd. *We're all just people,* Daniel reminded himself as Morty led them off the elevator and headed across the foyer. The restaurant was on the other side of it. *Nothing to see here, folks. Just four men going out for a bite to eat. Nothing unusual in that.*

Okay, so maybe they did stand out a bit. Zeke was six foot six, and Morty was roughly the same. Ty wasn't much shorter, and he stood out because of his natural grace and stunning looks. All the men had opted for suit pants and button down shirts for the evening and Zeke had taken the time to trim his beard. Walking briskly across the open area, heads did turn, but it wasn't as though any of them were recognizable from social media pictures. Daniel never posted any of himself.

There was a crowd milling around the restaurant entrance. Daniel spotted Saul and made out that he hadn't. Nothing was going to ruin his evening. But it seemed Saul had other ideas. "There he is," he heard Saul say clearly. "I met him this afternoon. The tall guy with the dark hair and the green shirt. That's D.B. Bear, everyone."

"What the fuck?" Zeke growled, but they didn't get a chance to say anything else before Ty was mobbed. Pulled away from his grip, all Daniel could do was stand and stare as readers pushed forward, some with books clasped to their chests, others with pieces of paper they wanted Ty to sign. All clamoring hello, and introducing themselves. Daniel recognized many of the names as his followers on Facebook.

"People, people, please," Ty said, backing up with a disarming grin. "I'm flattered, believe me, I am. But someone is playing a rather crude joke on you. I am not an author. I'm not D.B. Bear. I'm one of D.B. Bear's partners. That's all."

But no one was listening. Ty was being pushed back this time, surrounded by more and more people as they threw questions at him, asking about the next book, yelling out their favorite scenes, asking him to sign something and no matter how much Ty pushed away the books and things shoved under his nose, another one took its place. And all the while, Saul stood at the dining room entrance, a giant smirk on his face.

Zeke's fists were like giant clubs, and the snarl that ripped from his lips caused a momentary pause in the scene around Ty. But it was only momentary. "You did this," he growled, advancing on Saul.

"Stay here, little cub," Morty said quietly, making to go after his brother. "I'd better make sure no blood is shed."

But Daniel didn't want to stay. The crowds, although friendly were overwhelming; the noise, and the sinking realization that his readers would far rather believe someone like Ty wrote the stories they enjoyed than an insipid mouse like him was all too much. Using the confusion to his advantage, Daniel hurried back across the foyer and out into the street.

/~/~/~/~/

"You are an absolute asshole." Zeke got right in Saul's face. "Who the hell is running this convention thingy?"

"I don't know what you've got to complain about." Saul didn't back down. "So, your little ruse was found out. You're lucky I don't report you. Trying to pass off a pretty boy who's barely out of short pants as a respected author. Really? You've got to be kidding me. I know D.B. Bear." Saul tapped his own skinny chest. "I've spent hours communicating with him online. I know him like my own brother. We're connected. Soul mates."

"What do you know?" Morty asked quickly as Zeke struggled to contain his temper. Visions of Saul's head sticking out of the marble column by the door looked pretty good to him. "You claim to know him so well. You claim we're trying to perpetrate a fraud. What do you know, that tells you Ty Hollifield, is D.B. Bear?"

"I never said anything about a fraud," Saul said quickly. "But it's obvious, isn't it? That skinny little runt probably can't spell his own name. He's got no confidence, no class, no maturity. The man I spoke to, the man I *know*, is older, he has a wisdom about him. He understands the nuances of relationships, and creates the most fascinating worlds imaginable. He's the perfect man. He's that man." Saul pointed to Ty who had finally shaken off his followers and was headed in their direction.

"Where's Daniel?" Ty said urgently, ignoring Saul's look of lust. "I thought he was with you, but I can't find him in the foyer and he's not answering his phone."

"I told him to stay put, over there," Morty pointed to an empty space on the wall. "I guess the crowds got to him."

"Shit," Zeke shook his fist under Saul's nose. "This is all your fault.

You get the manager or organizer of this convention down here right this minute."

"D.B., Ty, can I call you Ty?" Saul said hopefully, peering around Zeke's large frame. "Look, I don't know what the issue is. So, I tumbled to your little ruse. You're so damn clever, I should've known you'd try something like this. But the secret's out now. Your fans deserve to know the real you, not some illiterate boy toy. Suck it up. Enjoy it. Your fans want to meet you. You can thank me in private later."

"Did he just call our precious Daniel illiterate?" Ty's eyebrows lowered. "Fuck this. Grab him, Z."

Zeke was more than happy to comply. Holding onto one arm each, he and his mate dragged Saul through the crowded foyer, towards the reception desk. A manager was hovering when they arrived, a look of concern on his face. "Is everything all right?" He asked, looking between

Zeke, Ty and Saul. "Has this man been causing a problem?"

"I'm Zeke McIntyre, this is my partner, Ty Hollifield. We demand to speak to the organizers of this convention. The people in charge."

"I'll see if Mr. Kirby's in his room. He and his husband organize this event every year." The manager picked up the phone, and tapped out a few numbers.

"Tell him this concerns the author, D.B. Bear," Zeke added when the call was clearly answered.

"You've done it now, Ty," Saul spat, still trying to get out of their hold. "Mr. Kirby's a big wig in this genre and I've got a lot of friends who read your books. You'd better let me go, or I'll see to it you'll never sell another story again."

"And that would probably bother me, if I wrote books for a living, which I don't. You, on the other hand, are party to creating a riot in the lobby of this fine hotel, and upsetting a dozen readers who think I'm someone I'm not, not to mention you've just threatened the livelihood of a respected member of this genre."

"Gentlemen, is there a problem here? I'm Graham Kirby, the organizer of this convention." A quiet voice sounded behind them, caused Zeke and Ty to turn, taking Saul with them.

"I want to lay a complaint," Zeke said firmly, shaking Saul's arm he was still holding. "My name is Zeke McIntyre, I run the Parkwood Hotel line. You may have heard of me. This is one of my partners, Ty Hollifield. You may know his name from Hollifield electronics. He's the owner of that company."

"I'm very pleased to meet such astute businessmen," Graham nodded his head slightly. "I've followed your company for years Mr. McIntyre and my husband and I have enjoyed many stays in your fine hotels. May I ask your issue is with my coordinator?"

"They're trying to pass off some pretty boy runt as the great author D.B. Bear." Saul yelled. "I was going to tell you, but I decided to let the readers make their own decisions. They can tell the truth a mile away."

"What truth is that, Saul?" Graham looked puzzled.

"That he is D.B. Bear." Wrestling out of Zeke's grip, Saul pointed at Ty. "They were trying to pass off an imposter. It would've been a huge scandal for the genre. So I called them out on it and I was right, because the guy who they told me was Bear, has up and disappeared."

"Mr. Hollifield, is this true? Do you write in your spare time? I imagine that would be quite an achievement if you did."

"It would be, if I was a writer, but I can assure you, my writing extends to compiling the monthly reports for my company and nothing else." Ty said grimly. "Our partner, Daniel is the author D.B. Bear, something Zeke and I are immensely proud of. We convinced him to attend this convention, thinking exposure to people who appreciated his work would be good for him. He's exceptionally shy."

"Instead," Zeke took up where Ty left off, "we were doubted the moment we set foot in this hotel. Your coordinator made Daniel feel as though he was a fraud from the moment he was introduced. He claims to have inside knowledge that proves Daniel isn't the author, and when we came downstairs to enjoy a quiet simple dinner as a threesome, well, four including my brother, this idiot yelled out across the foyer, describing *Ty* as the person our Daniel's fans were waiting for."

"Is this true, Saul?" Graham frowned. "And before you say anything that might make this worse, I've seen photos of Mr. McIntyre and Mr. Hollifield on their company reports, so I know they are who they say they are. I invest in their companies. Has D.B. Bear ever shared a picture of himself with you online? Because, I have to confess, gentlemen, I don't have a clue what he looks like."

"He's gorgeous," Zeke growled. "Well, Saul. Where's your proof? Show us the messages where the author described himself as six foot five, dark hair and green eyes instead of five foot six, blond hair and blue eyes."

"I don't have a picture," Saul muttered. "But anyone could see that blond was only fit to kneel in alleys and suck dick."

Words were not going to cut it this time. Zeke swung his fist, only remembering to pull back on his strength at the last minute. Even so, Saul flew over the reception desk and hit the floor on the other side with a groan. A flash of camera lights went off and Zeke mentally cursed. "He might need medical assistance," he muttered, peering over the reception counter to the slumped form on the floor.

"I'm sure you can see this whole incident has been very upsetting to Zeke and myself," Ty interjected quickly as Graham seemed unsure on what to do, although one of the receptionists was busy on the phone. "Our partner, Daniel is a kind, sweet and incredibly creative person. Saul's dismissal of him when we arrived was bad enough. His hoax, in creating a situation where innocent readers were busy telling *me* how wonderful his stories are, should've been something Daniel was being told. And thanks to that unconscious dickhead, our sweet partner lost that opportunity."

"Yes, well, I think if someone insulted my husband the way Saul did your Daniel, I'd like to think I'd have reacted in the same way." Graham tugged on his jacket. "Perhaps, if I could meet Daniel, we could work all this out without the police being involved? Daniel could probably sue Saul for slander, defamation of character and even fraud, and I'd understand if he'd want to. But there'll be roughly a thousand people who'd be very disappointed if D.B. Bear doesn't make his scheduled appearance on Friday."

"We have to find him first," Zeke said grimly. "He suffers from social anxiety and this will have hit him hard."

"I can sympathize with that too," Graham shook his head. "My husband Patrick suffers from the same complaint. It takes me a solid month to convince him to attend these things and we've been holding this event for seven years. I'll let you go and find him. Please let the reception know when he's been found, no matter what time it is. I'd like to meet this special young man for myself, at your convenience of course. I'll take care of matters here."

I'm not making any promises, Zeke thought as he, Morty and Ty hurried out of the hotel. After seeing what Ty was subjected to, with one informal meet and greet, Zeke was thinking yards of bubble wrap and a twenty four hour guard would be needed to keep his sweet Daniel safe.

Chapter Nineteen

Daniel hadn't gone far. For one thing, he didn't want to get lost getting back to the hotel, and for another, his bear wasn't keen on being apart from Zeke and Ty for too long. Trusting Zeke and Ty to work out the issue with his identification and that wretched Saul, Daniel decided to eat. He was dressed up, hungry, and besides, he had nothing better to do. The alien museum was closed. Ordering a huge hamburger and fries from a small café, three doors down from the hotel, Daniel checked his phone while sipping the coffee the friendly waitress had provided while the order was cooking.

Where are you? His friend Pat, who wrote under the name Dani Gray was messaging him.

Having dinner. He sent back. *Did you find Stormy okay?* Stormy Glenn, another author who wrote paranormal and contemporary MM stories, and Pat were close friends. He'd known, from the copious messages Pat had sent him, that they were looking forward to meeting up with each other and him at the conference. Living states apart, it wasn't easy to maintain friendships online, but those two managed it.

And they included me too, Daniel thought fondly. No matter how down he got, he could always rely on Pat to give him a pep talk. If he got stuck on a story, he could call her up and she'd come up with the craziest ideas. She was always ready with a smile and a laugh, and she was the most generous person Daniel had ever come across.

Stormy was the one who'd encouraged Daniel when he first started writing, although it was a few years before she realized what a huge influence she'd been on him. Her stories had inspired him to start writing. Now, he could message her anytime with questions, and she was always quick to answer. His whole system for keeping track of characters and story points came from her. Pat and Stormy were the only two people in his online acquaintance who knew what he looked like, but that was because neither one of them were shy about using video chat.

We're coming to you. Pat answered. *There's a big kerfuffle in the hotel foyer. I heard your name mentioned.*

I'm not there. Try the café three doors down. See if you recognize me in the flesh lol.

Hold a seat for us. Be there in five.

About to put his phone away, Daniel saw he'd missed a call from Ty's number. His mates would be worried, Daniel knew they would be, but he hoped, deep in his heart, that they'd understand too. His mates were big, strong, and positive stud muffins. They also had decades of experience in dealing with human conflicts. Daniel trusted Zeke to make sure Ty got out of the melee. He was also sure their uber sense of smell would hunt him down soon enough.

Looking up, Daniel didn't try to hide his smile as two women walked in. Pat's wild curly hair was streaked with rainbow colors and it seemed Stormy had gone for a rainbow wig in solidarity. "Oh my god," Pat yelled, turning more than one head in the small place, "look at you. You're so much smaller than you look on video."

"My image is probably distorted because I have a big computer screen," Daniel said standing up as the women approached. He wasn't ready for the hugs, but he should've been. While Stormy was quieter than her friend, they both knew how to deliver the best of Mom hugs. A hint of perfume, soft flesh, but it was the genuine kindness of his two friends that settled Daniel's nerves. "Sit down, sit down," he said when they finally released him. "I just ordered a burger and fries; did you want anything?"

"Coffee for me," Stormy said, sitting across from him. "The damn flight was two hours late and madam here has been talking my ear off since I arrived."

"It's just so exciting. We're all here together at last." Pat laughed. "I'll just have a Pepsi and fries. I had a meal on the plane."

Waving at the waitress, Daniel added to his order, but the waitress had barely left, when he saw his friends looking at him expectantly. "Well," Pat prompted. "What was all that kerfuffle back at the hotel? Why was your name being mentioned? Is that why you're here instead of drooling over those hotties I saw manhandling Saul?"

Oops. Daniel knew Zeke was angry, but hopefully Saul wasn't too badly hurt. "Saul took a dislike to me from the moment he met me in the flesh for some reason," Daniel shrugged as though it wasn't a big deal, although to him it was. "Then when me and my partners were going down to dinner, he caused a huge stampeded in the hotel lobby by telling some of my readers that one of my friends was D.B. Bear. They mobbed him. I slipped away."

"Aw, fuck hon, that had to hurt," Reaching over the table, Pat patted his hand. "I know you'd mentioned Saul's name before as one of your readers and close friends."

Stormy snorted. "That guy is a name dropper. He's been around since I started writing and that was a good ten years ago. Did I ever tell you, when I first started writing, he used to message me offering to help me write my sex scenes?"

"Eww, really?" Pat laughed. "Did you tell him you had a husband with a dick and you didn't need any help?"

Daniel laughed even as his cheeks flushed. "I suppose I should be grateful he never offered that to me. That would just be creepy."

"Enough about him," Pat said leaning on the table. "Come on, spill the beans. Don't think we missed the part where you said partners. You've been single forever. Is that partners in the collaborative sense, or the fun kind of partners."

Daniel tensed for a moment. Pat and Stormy weren't shifters even though they wrote about them. To his best friends, his world was fictional and while they'd understand the concepts of mates, they wouldn't imagine it happening in their real life. "I have life partners," he said, trying not to smile. "Life partners as in two men who've moved in with me and now share my life in all ways."

"Oh, my gods, you horn dog!" Pat laughed. "I know I told you to get our more and taste some dick, but two of them? Which ones, which ones? Did we see them in the lobby?"

"There were two bald guys with beards, and another tall sexy dreamboat talking to the manager of the hotel when we came through. They had that Saul creep with them," Stormy added.

"The two bald guys are brothers," Daniel grinned at Pat's shocked expression, "and no, I am not with the brothers. Just one of them and the dreamboat."

"Oh, man, could you imagine one of those beards tickling your inner thighs." Leaning back in her chair, Pat fanned herself with the menu.

"You're married," Stormy chuckled, elbowing her friend in the ribs.

"I'm not dead," Pat said firmly. "Twenty odd years I've been with my hubby, but that doesn't stop my mind working. Those hunks are built in all the right places. Besides, drooling is not touching. Hubby knows where I sleep and who I sleep with, since I can never get a decent sleep unless he's right next to me."

"Yes, well, your sleeping arrangements aside, they're my hunks," Daniel said with a wink. "I imagine they'll come looking for me soon, so I'll introduce you then."

The waitress chose that moment to deliver the food and drinks ordered. Daniel took a huge bite of his burger, carefully wiping the excess sauce from his chin.

"Are you okay with being here?" Stormy asked quietly after he'd eaten about half of his burger. "You've mentioned about being a bit anxious in gatherings and things like that. You blew us off last year. You know, I found that picture you sent us of your ankle in a cast on a stock photography site, but I didn't say anything because I figured you had good reason for not coming."

Daniel put down his burger. "I am sorry about lying to you. I just couldn't face it all – the travel, the worry, it got too much for me."

"Then it's a good thing you found those hunks of yours," Pat said. "They might drag you out to these things a bit more often."

"How do you cope with it? All the attention I mean," Daniel asked. "You both have huge followings…."

"Hers more than ours, right?" Pat grinned at Stormy. "She's the one who's been writing smut since she could work out what a computer was for."

"Exactly," Daniel agreed. "When those people in the lobby thought Ty was me, they got right in his face, all wanting to talk to him at once, not letting him get a word in."

"It's because D.B. Bear is all dark and mysterious," Stormy waggled her hands for emphasis. "Once people know who you are, they won't make such a big deal. But you've been writing, what? Five years? And no one has ever seen your face, except us."

"Because we're special," Pat wiggled her eyebrows. "But enough about that. How did you meet your two incredible hunks if you barely leave the house? Inquiring minds want to know."

Chapter Twenty

"Daniel's in here." Morty, who was leading the search because he had the strongest sense of smell, stopped outside a small, cheery café. "And he's not alone. I thought you said he didn't talk to people."

Peering through the window, Ty saw Daniel tilt his head back and laugh at something one of the women he was with said. "He's mentioned video chatting with a couple of ladies a few times since we've met him. Maybe that's who the women are? At least they're not giving him grief about the way he looks."

"How that fucking Saul could relegate our sweet Daniel to someone who sucks dick in an alley makes me furious," Zeke seethed. "All the work he's done, all the wonderful stories he's written, and that guy has the gall to call him illiterate."

"Jealousy, bro, plain and simple," Morty said, slapping his hand on

Zeke's shoulder. "You look at your cub. He's gorgeous, smart, funny, and stands out in a crowd. You heard Saul, he called Daniel his soul mate. Clearly, Saul was more hung up on looks that he let on."

"The danger of the internet," Ty agreed. "Daniel said there were no photos of him online at all, and I checked. He's right. So, even if Saul asked for one, Daniel didn't send it. Knowing Saul and his vivid imagination, he probably thought Daniel was interested in him romantically."

"Yeah, well are we going to stand around here hovering or go in?" Zeke scowled. "I need to make sure he's all right."

Instead of answering, Ty opened the door. Daniel had been waiting for them. It was clear the way he immediately looked up, his eyes sparkling. Ty's heart melted. "I told you they'd come and look for me when they were done," Daniel said to the women at the table. "Now, you can meet them for yourself, but keep your drooling to a minimum."

The woman with the rainbow colors in her hair immediately turned around in her seat, her mouth dropping open. "Damn, they are even finer close up. Quick, come sit by me, so I can bask in your studly glory." She dragged a chair over and set it close to her own, patting the seat.

Daniel made the introductions. "Ladies, these are my partners, Ty and Zeke, and Zeke's brother Mortimer. Guys, allow me to introduce Pat and Stormy, fellow authors and my two closest friends."

"Obviously, good friends," Ty murmured, "they know what you look like." Grabbing chairs of their own, Zeke and Ty made sure they were sitting on either side of Daniel, while Mortimer grinned and took the chair next to Pat.

"Ladies, it's an honor to meet you," Morty said with a nod. "Have you been to many of these events before. What can you tell us about them? It's our first time."

Grateful Morty was doing a wonderful job of distracting Daniel's friends, Ty leaned over the back of Daniel's chair. "Are you okay? You took ten years off our lives, disappearing the way you did."

"I knew you'd find me. I didn't go running for home," Daniel said with a hesitant smile. "I trusted you two to handle the situation and kept myself safe until you could get to me. I'm just sorry you got mobbed like that. I didn't realize so many people would be keen to meet D.B. Bear."

"It's all anyone could talk about on social media," Stormy chipped in, clearly overhearing. "You wouldn't have seen it, as you've been offline, but the excitement is huge."

"Yep, but you don't have to worry now," Pat said, banging her fist on the table. "Anyone gives you any grief like that idiot Saul will have their heads bashed in."

"I think Zeke already took care of Saul. He's going to have a bruised jaw in the morning," Ty laughed as Zeke did some sweet murmuring of his own in Daniel's ear. Ty wasn't sure what his big mate was saying, but Daniel's cheeks were a lovely shade of pink.

"The people here are good people," Stormy said. "Honestly, I've been coming to these things for years, and apart from the odd rivalry between authors, it's a really fun event. Readers want to get the chance to get to know their favorite authors better and they are always so supportive. Daniel just happens to have a lot of readers who consider him their favorite."

"We can still go home, Daniel, you only have to say the word." Ty understood what Stormy was saying, but that full on mob worried him for a moment, and he was a lot bigger than their sweet cub.

"No, you can't go, Daniel," Pat protested. "You've just got here, and there's so much going on over the next three days. Come on, please stay. You have to see mine and Stormy's outfits for the party. I worked on my jacket for weeks."

"The ones you told me about online the other day?" Daniel grinned as he took Ty's hand under the table. "So long as no one makes a big deal about my relationship with my partners, I'll stay. If one person upsets them in any way, then we'll leave. Besides, I want to see the alien museum, it might give me some ideas."

"If anyone says the slightest negative thing about you and your hunks, we'll throw Morty at them." Stormy and Pat crossed their arms over their chest and glared while Morty burst out laughing.

"Glad I can be of some service ladies," Morty said with a gallant bow.

"Ty, tell Stormy how you felt about The Hot Mess series, and Pat, she writes as Dani Gray. You read Cupid's Valentine, didn't you?"

"Sure did." Apart from Daniel, Ty had never been in a position of being able to talk to an author about their stories before. But as more food was ordered, coffee flowed, and laughter rang around the table, he had to agree it was a lot of fun. Daniel had his legs on Zeke's lap, and was leaning hard on Ty's shoulder. They were in public, relaxed and happy. It was exactly the outcome Ty hoped for when he'd forced the issue about the trip. *All we have to do now, is make sure things stay this way.*

/~/~/~/~/

"I'll be up in a minute," Zeke waved his mates and brother onto the elevator, and then headed back to the reception desk as soon as the elevator door was closed. "Is Mr. Kirby available?" He asked the receptionist who was manning the desk alone. The lobby was quiet, the lights dimmed. They'd been at the café for longer than he'd thought.

"He left word for us to contact him, the moment you came in, Mr. McIntyre." The young lady leaned over the desk, looking left and right before she whispered, "That man you hit has been kicking up a song and dance about wanting to lay charges against you. Mr. Kirby's managed to hold him off for now, telling the police who were called that you'd been severely provoked, suggesting that the whole thing was a hate crime, which made the smaller guy back off. I believe Mr. Kirby was hoping the man would check out, but he insisted on staying, even though he won't be allowed into any of the conference events."

Shit and double shit. The last thing Zeke wanted was for Saul to upset any of Daniel's new found confidence. "I appreciate you letting me know," he said quietly. "Can you see if Mr. Kirby is free? I'd understand if he didn't want to speak with me until morning. I didn't realize how late it had gotten."

"Neither Mr. Kirby or his husband will get much sleep the next few days," the receptionist smiled. "That's why we don't mind hosting the event. They stay on top of everything. Excuse me a moment."

She moved over to the phone. Zeke turned and rested his back and elbows on the reception counter. In hindsight, hitting Saul was a dumb thing to do. *Correction,* Zeke thought, *it was a dumb thing hitting him in public with a dozen human witnesses around.* Zeke had very few run-ins with police. He and Ty dressed and acted like bikers a lot of the time, but they never did anything illegal. Bears did not do well in confinement, and besides the people who did pick fights with either of them, weren't the type to call the police. *I wonder if it's time to call my lawyer?*

"Mr. Kirby said it was fine for you to go up to their room – 549 – the suite underneath yours." The receptionist smiled, and Zeke was quick to return it as a professional courtesy, but his mind was racing as he headed for the elevators. Hopefully, Kirby would have a better idea of how much trouble he was in.

Chapter Twenty One

"How bad is it?" Daniel asked, sitting on the edge of the couch. "Did you and Zeke get into any trouble over this business with Saul? I assume that's why our mate didn't come upstairs with us?" The evening spent with Pat and Stormy had been hilarious fun – Daniel didn't think he'd ever laughed as much in his life. But as soon as he walked through the lobby, his bear went on alert. Morty had stayed in town – he wanted to follow a *feeling* – so for the moment, Ty and Daniel were alone.

"Babe, the one thing you don't have to do is worry about Zeke." Ty came over, dropping down beside him. "Yes, technically, under the law, Zeke committed assault on Saul, but it was one punch and the guy was only out for a few minutes. He's going to have a wicked bruise and a headache, but that's all."

"Z punched him, in front of all those people?" Fuck, it was worse than

Daniel thought. "His bear will go crazy if he has to go to jail."

"I doubt any jail time will be involved," Ty said gently. "There were a dozen witnesses, aside from us, who'd testify how hateful, insulting and potentially damaging Saul's words were. He threatened your career."

The last thing Daniel was thinking about was his career. His guts were twisted, his heart pounding at the thought of the police arresting his mates. "Do you think it would help if I talked to Saul, online maybe? I can't work out why he's suddenly hating me on sight."

"When was the last time you were messaging him?" Ty sprawled out, resting his feet on the coffee table, his arm lifted for Daniel to scoot under. Daniel couldn't refuse the invitation. Settling against Ty's chest, he pulled out his phone and tapped into his messenger program.

"There's nothing in his messages suggesting he didn't like me or my work," Daniel said, finding the message thread. "See, we were chatting last week. He said he was flat out busy helping Graham with the conference, and couldn't wait to meet me in person." Ty reached over, plucking the phone from his hands, using his thumb to scroll the screen.

"Is it normal for your readers to call you babe and sweet cheeks?" Ty quirked an eyebrow.

"No," Daniel protested, feeling his cheeks heat up. "My good friends, like Pat and Stormy know my name is Daniel, but very few others do. I don't think it ever came up in conversation with Saul, but then from what he said, he uses those terms with everyone, it's just his way of being friendly. It's better than calling me D.B or Mr. Bear."

"I'm not so sure it is." Ty was quiet for a moment, scrolling through the messages. "You do know what flirting looks like, don't you? Your characters do it often enough."

"Saul wasn't flirting with me, not like he did with you, when we arrived," Daniel said hotly, stung his mate thought he was completely socially inept.

"There're different types of flirting," Ty frowned at the screen. Daniel wished he hadn't shown it to him now. "This here, about a month ago, where he's going on about how the two of you could write a great love story together."

"Book ideas." Daniel frowned, vaguely remembering the messages. "I talk to a lot of authors about different plot ideas – it's a great way of boosting creativity when I'm stuck, and a lot of authors find it helpful when they aren't sure what they're going to write next."

"I don't think that's what Saul had in mind," Ty said slowly. "The premise of the story – a reader and author meet at a conference and fall in love despite the odds. Doesn't it sound too coincidental to you?"

"Oh, that was a contemporary story he was talking about. He knows I only write paranormal romances, but he still brings it up every now and then. I was just encouraging his ideas. From memory, he did go on about it a bit."

"More than go on about it – he was quoting full scenes in this imaginary story." Looking up, Daniel saw Ty's eyes had narrowed and his lips were a tight line.

"It's just story ideas," he said gently, running his palm down Ty's thigh. "I've discussed heaps of different concepts with authors, including murder, alien abduction and slavery. I don't write about things like that and I don't ever plan on doing anything like that in real life, and neither do the people I talk to. Sharing plot twists helps writers feel connected with another likeminded person, that's all it is."

"Daniel, he describes a full sex scene between the reader and the author."

Daniel winced. Ty rarely used his name and Daniel had gotten used to being called babe, among other things.

"His book is just in the planning stages, he wanted advice on his writing style and sent me a couple of scenes, so I could comment on them."

"I can see what he says, but didn't anything about that scene strike you as strange?"

"There was no growling, roaring or biting involved?" Daniel worried his bottom lip with his teeth. "I doubt I was paying much attention to the content. I told you, he was asking me about his writing style – his voice, and how it came across on the page."

"That's bullshit. Look at these descriptions. Samuel, the reader, is described as five eight, dark hair, dark eyes, and a slender figure. There is also a lot of mention about the man's oversized, well-proportioned, and various other terms along the same vein concerning his dick."

"That could be any number of fictional men."

"Dirk Beard – note the D.B initials - is described as six foot four, long dark hair, pale green eyes and a body that won't quit. In contrast to the numerous adjectives describing Samuel's junk, Dirk's dick size is considered 'proportionate'."

"Dirk sounds a lot like you, although I wouldn't use the word proportionate to describe your dick – there's a lot of better things I could say about that," Daniel said as his hand trailed higher up Ty's thigh. Ty reached down, catching his hand before he got to the enticing bulge he was aiming for.

"Daniel, the man was describing a scene between himself and his ideal of you. Listen to this, the supposed opening scene." Ty flicked through the messages for a moment, and then started to read. "The hotel lobby was busy, readers and authors alike, checking in, greeting old friends, introducing themselves to new ones. Samuel hovered by the entrance, clutching his clipboard tightly. Dirk was late, but that was to be expected. The author was flying in from the other side of the country. Tugging on his jacket, Samuel then pulled his phone out of the pocket. No messages yet. Oh, my gods, this bit is in italics indicating a direct thought," Ty added, "Oh my gods, I get to meet my future today."

Frowning, Daniel rubbed the lines on his forehead. His gut twisted, threatening to eject the burger he'd eaten earlier. "Go on."

"There's blah, blah, blah about how the two of them had never even exchanged photographs, but how Samuel already fancied himself in love with the caring, mature author. They'd exchanged so many secrets, and Dirk had mentioned more than once how lonely the life of an author could be. I'll read this next bit."

Daniel wasn't sure he wanted to hear it.

"There was a commotion at the door. A tall man, with a commanding air, swept into the lobby and looked around. Samuel's mouth dropped open. His cock twitched, and his heart rate sped up. The tall man's eyes caught his. They were green, just as Samuel imagined. A small smile tugged at the handsome man's full lips before he said, 'Samuel'. Dropping his clipboard, Samuel ran into the man's open arms. Hot lips scorched his...." Ty trailed off in disgust. "You get the picture."

It took a moment for Daniel to connect the dots. "You think," he said hesitantly, "you think Saul was writing a story about a meeting between himself as the reader and Dirk as me? At this conference?" Daniel's voice rose at the end.

"Isn't it obvious." Ty's voice was flat.

"So, when he saw you, he thought his fantasies had come to life?" Daniel couldn't believe it. "For fucks sake, it was a story idea. There's no way Saul could've known I'd mated to a man who filled his ideal fantasy. I was originally coming alone, or so Saul thought, and you heard him when we met – he used they and their pronouns. He thought I was a woman."

"No, you thought Saul thought you were a woman. He was probably being truthful when he said he refers to any author that way. But he guessed you were a man. These fantasies are far too detailed to suggest anything else. And you encouraged him!"

Spinning around in his seat, Daniel poked Ty's chest with his finger. "You can read what I said. Oh, that's nice, good idea, you should keep writing. I was encouraging his story, not his fantasies. Don't put this on me. I've messaged the same thing to Stormy, Pat and some of my other author friends hundreds of times."

"Daniel, the man wants you. He's been lusting over D.B. Bear for months." Daniel's frown deepened as Ty's hands landed heavily on his shoulders. He shrugged them off.

"Actually, if you're going to be pedantic about this, it's not me he wants, it's you," Daniel snapped back. "And you're the one who told me this trip was such a good idea. You're the one who pulled me from my home, where I was safe and told me you'd protect me. So, I don't fit his ideal man image? Woo fucking hoo. I was never interested in him that way anyway. Maybe you're the one who should be watching your ass, but don't you dare start blaming me for this. I'm not responsible for the sick things that goes on in Saul's head, he is."

"How cute, you do have a brain in your head after all. Unfortunately, that won't save you now," a chilling voice sounded by the elevator door. Turning his head, Daniel gasped as he saw Saul standing with a gun pointed right at him. Before he could react, a shot rang out and a searing pain blossomed in the top of his chest. Clutching the sudden hole that appeared, Daniel's eyelids fluttered as warm blood poured over his fingers. Vomiting was a real threat now as the pain spread. Reaching out to Ty, Daniel knew he wasn't going to make it. The dark spots before his eyes converged and he fell sideways on the couch. Then there was nothing.

Chapter Twenty Two

"I'm going to kill you for this," Ty promised Saul, as he leaned over Daniel's prone body, reaching around his back to see if the bullet had come through the other side. Daniel's sexy blue shirt was covered in blood, but there was no exit wound. Ty knew, from experience, if the bullet wasn't removed quickly, Daniel's shifter healing was going to make the experience a lot more uncomfortable.

"I really wouldn't bother trying to save him," Saul said with a dark chuckle. "Besides, we've got more important things to talk about, like why you tried to deceive me and everyone else, trying to pass off that ridiculous twink as an international bestselling author."

"I can prove Daniel is who he claims to be," Ty said tersely, ripping Daniel's shirt away from the wound. "Can you prove he's not?" *Keep the mad man talking. Where the fuck is Z?* Using the edge of the ripped shirt,

Ty wiped away some of the blood. As he suspected, the wound was already healing over which created a double problem. If Saul saw it, there'd be hell to pay, and if Ty didn't get that bullet out, the wound would need to be opened up again to get it out. Grabbing the torn shirt into a bunch, he pressed it so the wound was hidden from Saul while trying to maneuver his finger into it. *I'm so glad you conked out, sweetness. This is going to hurt like a bitch.*

"Will you stop fussing with that rent boy," Saul edged closer waving his gun. "You read that beautiful scene I wrote just for you. I heard you talking about it. So, why did you have to go and spoil the real thing? I've been waiting for that magical moment between us for months, ever since I knew you were confirmed to come to the conference."

"Don't you know the difference between real life and fiction?" Ty risked a quick look at Saul, while trying to focus his bear enough to shift one claw. His Kodiak was battling his instincts – care for his mate and kill the bastard responsible for the blood. A full blown paw couldn't be hidden... Ty needed just one claw. *Come on, bear, co-operate with me. Phew, finally....*

"We connected on a soul deep level and when I saw you, I knew our dreams would come true," Saul insisted. He was so close Ty could reach out and punch him, which would be awkward given he was claw deep in his mate's wound at the time. "I know you felt it too. The long chats, the shared interests. You loved every one of the samples I sent you."

"And what did you think of D.B. Bear's stories?" *Would you just fuck off and let me care for my mate?*

"What?" Saul seemed surprised Ty even asked. "Oh, I get what you're doing. Trying to divert me, still making out you didn't write those books, by talking about yourself in the third person. Look, the books are okay, if you're into shifter stuff, but personally, I get bored with all that roaring and mine that goes on all the time. But there's no reason we can't write a contemporary story together with the concepts of soul mates. Honestly, it'll sell to a much larger audience and be far more plausible than anything you've put out before."

"Hang on a minute. Are you telling me, you don't even like D.B. Bear's books? What about the Everlast series?" Ty grunted. He had his claw hooked around the bullet, but Daniel's skin was healing around him with every passing second. He had to pull it out without causing any more internal injuries. Holding his breath, Ty slowly wiggled his claw out of Daniel's chest, pulling the bullet with it.

"Don't you get it; shifter books are so last year. Chest beating alphas throwing each other up against the wall, yelling 'mine' if someone even looks at their mates the wrong way. How the hell are we going to live comfortable lives together if you can't write books people will actually buy?"

"The readers seem to love Daniel's bears." *Yes, got it out,* and what's more, Ty could hear the elevator, his bear recognizing Zeke was near. And his mate wasn't alone. Shit, this was going to be awkward. Someone must have heard the shot fired, but Daniel was basically healed. There was nothing but a pink round mark where the bullet hole used to be. His teeth clenched at the thought of hurting his mate, Ty used his claw, drawing a long deep gash across the top of Daniel's shoulder. Hopefully that would pass as a graze from a bullet and it would be covered quickly, because damn, as an Omega, Daniel healed fast.

"Bear shifters aren't believable, any form of shifter is just bullshit," Saul insisted. *Why was this asshole still talking?* "Who on earth, in their right mind, would believe a man could turn into a bear at will?"

"I would." His mate was slowly coming around, there were people coming who could get hurt, and Saul still had the gun. Ty raised his finger, still shifted into a claw and waved it in front of Saul's face. "Say goodnight, asshole."

Saul's mouth opened but anything he was going to say was lost as Ty swung his fist, knocking the man to the floor, the gun skidding across the carpet. Suddenly the room was full of people, police, hotel management, Mr. Kirby and another man who could easily be his twin. But all Ty saw and felt was Zeke. The man was trembling as he grabbed hold of them both and for the longest moment, Ty just focused on breathing in his mate's wonderful scent.

/~/~/~/~/

The chat with Graham and Patrick had been going well. Graham was just concerned Zeke and his mates, in particular Daniel, would leave the conference before it had started properly. Graham was busy explaining the benefits the conference gave to authors and readers alike when they all heard it – the sound of a gunshot coming from the room above.

"Damn it, they left the elevator unlocked for me. Someone's got up there." Zeke jumped to his feet, rushing for the door.

"We should wait for police back up." Patrick already had his phone out. He looked a lot like his husband, but didn't say a lot.

"I'll call the hotel manager," Graham added. "They've probably got a policy on how to handle things like this."

Zeke knew all about hotel policy. Heading upstairs without back up, something a sensible human would wait for, wasn't an option. Pacing the floor, he fumed over their lack of mind link. His bear knew Daniel had been hurt, but wasn't dead, but that was cold comfort when every cell in his body wanted to be with his mates. *Who? What? Why?* A million variations on the basic questions, none of which were being answered, because he was standing around in a hotel suite pretending to be human.

Which was why, when they finally got the okay to go upstairs, Zeke wasn't afraid to use his bulk, pushing aside the police who were trying to hold him back, so he could get out of the elevator first. He could smell Daniel's blood the moment the elevator door opened along with the acrid smell of a gun recently fired. Ty was huddled over his mate's prone body with blood on his hands, Saul was passed out on the floor, a dark bruise forming across his jaw. Stepping over the asshole responsible for the shot, Zeke gathered his mates up close to his chest, making a silent vow that the mind link issue was

going to be resolved before they got
any sleep at all.

Chapter Twenty Three

"Please, please, please, please," Daniel begged, his neck arched, his body strung tight. The police were gone, taking Saul and the gun with them. The bandage the paramedics insisted he wear on his shoulder was ripped off as soon as everyone had left. The elevator door was locked and the sexual tension in the air could be cut with a knife. He was scar free, with just an ache in his chest where the bullet had gone, and cleaned up. He'd even eaten, but now, when things could and should get hot and heavy, his mates were being damn stubborn about filling his hole and giving his cock the friction it badly needed.

"If you move, we'll stop," Zeke rumbled before leaning back down to capture Daniel's nipple in his mouth. His gruff tone let Daniel know he wasn't kidding, but Daniel didn't understand why his mates were torturing him. He felt the same need to connect with his lovers as they did. He'd woken up to find himself in Zeke's lap, while Ty was speaking with police. Nothing would convince Zeke to let him go, not then, not now, but damn it, the man's cock was digging in his thigh. A slight movement up and to the left about three inches and Daniel could get what he wanted.

"You can't always have things your own way," Ty observed, moving up to nibble around Daniel's neck. "Zeke and I think it's high time things were changed up a bit."

Changed up? How the hell are they even talking like it was just another day. I've had a near death experience here. I'm horny, desperate, I need to reconnect with my mates. But all Daniel could do was moan. His ability to form words had ended ten minutes before when Zeke pressed his thick thumbs into the soles of Daniel's left foot and started sucking his toes. Ty working on his right side. And so, it had gone, licking and nibbling their way up his body. Wonderful, stupendous, and so damn frustrating because even though his cock leaned to the left, Zeke missed it completely and Ty couldn't be encouraged to swap sides no matter how much Daniel tried to wiggle his hips in that direction.

"Pass me the lube, babe." Daniel heard the snick of the lube tube. His body tensed, waiting for that delicious moment when blunt fingers and stickiness prodded, then breached his body. But the expected fingers never came. Daniel opened his eyes to see Ty preparing Zeke's ass. His groan was of frustration this time.

"Guys, no fair," Daniel panted. He'd only seen Ty take Zeke once in their short time together, and while it was hot, seeing his biker mate reduced to a muttering wreck as Ty plundered his body, he'd been so sure they'd both want to fuck him this time. He was the one who'd been shot –

shouldn't they be driven by their animal forms to have proof of life/celebratory sex with him?

"I told you we were switching things up." Ty flashed him a wink and a smirk. "You ready?"

For what? For fuck's sake... ahhhhhhhhh. Daniel closed his eyes in sheer relief. Ty's hand was wrapped around his cock at last, holding it away from his body. Daniel would work with that. A bit of a wiggle, a few thrusts... "What the fuck?" That wasn't Ty's mouth enclosing the head of his dick. His eyes flying open, Daniel looked up to see Zeke lowering himself on Daniel's cock. "Stop!"

"Really?" Zeke grumbled as he froze. "You want to stop now?"

"Yes." Zeke levered up slightly and the pressure on his cock head eased. "No!" Daniel moaned. "I don't know how to do this. I could hurt you."

"Is that the only thing bothering you about doing things this way?" Ty asked. Daniel noticed he was stroking his own cock in long slow moves.

"I've done the research," At least shock had shoved the need to climax to the back of Daniel's mind. "You can't just shove a dick in a hole and start pounding." Okay, his tone might have had a pleading edge. Daniel feared and longed to top his mates just once.

"Have you been reading anal sex horror story forums?" Ty shook his head. "Babe, I thought you knew you can't believe everything you read on the internet."

"But... but..."

"Yes, it's true to a point," Ty took pity on him. "Some people just don't enjoy anyone or anything near their ass and there's nothing wrong with those feelings – we're all different. And yes, if one of those people 'tried' to bottom, maybe to please a lover, then the tension in their body alone can cause the whole experience to be painful. But babe, we've been doing this since before you were born."

"You don't have much control over the thrusting side of things with me being on top like this," Zeke explained. "I control how far and how fast you penetrate me."

Leaning over, Ty brushed the hair out of Daniel's eyes. "It is so damn sweet that you worry about hurting us, but babe, after what we went through today, Zeke and I both agreed we need that mind link. If we had…" He trailed off, but Daniel understood. He'd lost count of the number of times he wished they could speak to each other telepathically. The evening's episodes were just one on a long list of times.

"Are you positive I won't hurt you?" Daniel studied Zeke's face.

"I won't let you. Trust us," Zeke whispered as he gently lowered himself back down again. Daniel was riveted by the strength and power in his mate's thighs. Rock solid, they didn't even tremble. Reaching out tentatively, he ran his palms over the glistening skin, keeping a close eye on Zeke's expression as the man bottomed out. Zeke's rumbling sigh lit the fire under Daniel's balls again and he gritted his teeth, determined to give Zeke some pleasure.

Oh, but his determination to please his lover was sorely tested as Zeke rolled his hips. Pressure unlike anything else he'd felt before, surrounded his cock, pulsating as if determined to drain Daniel's balls dry. Leaning forward slightly, dropping his hands on the mattress on either side of Daniel's head, Zeke groaned as he started to slowly rock up and down. Daniel felt that groan reverberate with his own. Instinct was taking over, Daniel's bear, who was usually slept when he was intimate with his mates, was wide awake and pushing forward. The grizzly was excited and proud, eager to claim his stunning alphas. Zeke changed his angle yet again, letting out a deep rumble as he moved faster.

"Give into your instincts," Ty murmured beside him. "Let your bear do his thing."

Like Daniel had any choice. Usually meek, mild and laid back, the grizzly seemed to know exactly what to do. As Zeke bent himself almost in half, presenting his neck, Daniel felt his fangs drop and without even thinking about it, he bit into the tight muscle, groaning as the unfamiliar taste of blood hit his tongue. One swallow, and then another, and Daniel pulled his teeth free, having just enough time to lick the wound before his orgasm threw his body into a spasm. Zeke roared. Hot spunk coated Daniel's stomach and chest.

Connection. Even though the grizzly knew he still had one more mate to bite, the connection with Zeke was intense. Daniel could feel the Kodiak's pleasure at being claimed, the deep sense of contentment – the sense of coming home. A bit of a shuffle, a few pulls on his dick and Ty took Zeke's place. Five minutes later, Daniel's back to back orgasms had wiped him out. He fell asleep, covered in his mate's ejaculate, safe and secure with the twin buzzes lodged in the back of his brain. His bear's sudden craving for blueberries would have to wait.

/~/~/~/~/

We did it, babe. Throwing the washcloth in the direction of the bathroom, Zeke pulled Ty closer to his chest, his mate's beautiful voice sounding loud and clear in his head. *Our days of seeking are finally over. We have a home, our sweet young cub and we're finally claimed in every way...*

The new chapter in our lives can begin in earnest now. Zeke sent back. Ty's delighted shiver and the way he burrowed even closer, lulling him into sleep.

Chapter Twenty Four

None of them saw a lot of the conference. Zeke was able to claim, with a completely straight face, that the shooting incident had badly shaken the young author and everyone, for the most part, gave them the space they needed to further their bond, which they did vigorously and often. Pat and Stormy stopped by the second night, showing off their outfits for the big party, and filling Daniel in on all the gossip.

Apparently, he hadn't been the only author targeted so persistently by the delusional Saul, although he was the only one who'd been shot at. The police informed them Saul would be spending the next few years in jail at least. Zeke and Ty's matching glowers had Daniel thinking the man would probably get more if their high-priced lawyers had anything to do with it. He was just thankful that Saul was taking a plea deal, so Daniel didn't have to testify.

Daniel missed the Q and A session too. While he knew Saul was an isolated case, and a fruitcake, he wasn't ready to face random questions from his readers, especially when everyone seemed to have their own ideas of what happened with him and Saul. Pat, the dear friend that she was, offered to fill in for him and had a wonderful time telling stories about him to a packed room, which she informed the audience with an evil cackle afterwards were entirely made up, 'because that's what fiction writers do'.

The one thing Daniel agreed to do, just after Ty and Zeke had sucked the brains out of his cock, was give his speech. The last speaker slot at the conference was a highly coveted spot, but the other authors due to speak all agreed, even though they'd never met him, to give Daniel that honor. Which was why, with his arm heavily bandaged, and resting in a sling, even though none of it was needed, Daniel was waiting with his mates in the back area of the conference room stage, to be announced.

"Now, you've got your notes?" Ty patted his jacket pocket. "Here, let me straighten that tie."

"There's still time for us to get a chair out there for you," Zeke chimed in. "Graham did offer – he's worried you might feel faint."

"You and I both know that the only reason I might possibly faint is because of nerves or the fact you both pounded me into the mattress half an hour ago," Daniel hissed.

"Made you a lot more relaxed though," Ty grinned, stepping back after finishing with his tie. "You look amazing."

Daniel blinked back the sudden onset of tears – his anxiety had a lot to answer for. He hadn't been able to eat a thing all morning, but that didn't stop his guts from churning as though they were processing a three course meal. "If they laugh at me, I swear I'm never coming to one of these things again."

"They won't laugh, and we'll be right here waiting for you," Zeke promised. "The bikes are packed and as soon as you come off the stage we're heading out."

"Home?" Daniel asked hopefully.

"For a few weeks." Ty and Zeke shared glances. "We were hoping we might be able to convince you to come with us on a sponsored bike run heading out from Austin at the end of the month," Ty admitted. "It's a Toys for Children drive."

"I'm sure you've got numerous ways of persuading me, when we get home." Daniel had a sudden thought. "Hey, what happened to Morty? I haven't seen him since we met Pat and Stormy at the café. I thought he'd be here for my speech at least."

"I've had one text from him," Zeke shrugged. "Following a feeling, so the text said. But don't worry about him.

He's got our new address and before you know it, he'll be on our doorstep looking for a place to crash for a few days."

Daniel's worry must have shown on his face. "He'll be fine," Ty promised. "Morty's the last person to do anything rash or stupid. He's a big boy. He can take care of himself. Now, are you ready? I see Graham is about to announce you."

There is no way in a month of Sundays I'm ready for this. Daniel wasn't sure his feet could even move, and he clutched the note cards tightly in his sweaty hands.

"The internet has opened up a lot of opportunities for would-be writers to showcase their work," Graham said, his voice loud thanks to the microphone. "Hundreds of people say they'd like to write a book one day. A tenth of them actually start writing. But it is only one percent of those people who have a story idea who finally finish their first book. The percentage of people who go on to carve a career out of what they love is smaller than that again. Imagine that, less than one percent. We are really privileged this morning to hear from a young man who self-published his first book at the tender age of eighteen years old. Now, five years later, D.B. Bear has gone on to write a further twenty stories covering four exciting series."

Cheers and clapping assaulted Daniel's ears as soon as his name was mentioned. Graham motioned them to be quiet. "D.B. Bear has captured our imaginations with his colorful and vibrant characters, his exciting plots, and most of all showing that there is a love for everyone, no matter who they might be. Acclaimed author of the Everlast series, I am proud to announce, for his first time ever in a public appearance, D.B. Bear. Come on out, Daniel."

Graham held out his hand and somehow Daniel found himself moving forward. He wasn't sure if it was Zeke or Ty who pushed him. Terrified he would trip on the stage, Daniel kept his eyes on Graham, who was clapping wildly. Out of the corner of his eye, he spotted Pat and Stormy in the front row, still wearing their rainbow hair, jumping up and down and cheering wildly.

"They're all yours," Graham whispered kindly as Daniel stepped up to the podium. "Imagine them naked."

That will not help in this case. Putting his notes on the podium, Daniel lifted his head. The room was packed. Some faces he recognized from social media photos, others he didn't. Inhaling slowly, Daniel forced a smile. "Wow. It looks like you've all had a really good time over the past few days. I'm only sorry," he lifted his arm in the sling, "I wasn't able to participate more this time around."

"We love you, Daniel," a voice came from the back.

"I love you all too," Daniel said honestly and somehow, that simple vote of confidence let him open his mouth and speak. "The world of fiction is a marvelous thing. Authors, like myself sit alone in our offices or anywhere we can put a laptop, tapping into overactive minds, creating stories one word at a time. The urge to clutch our precious finished books to our chest, hiding them away and never letting them see the light of day, is strong in all writers. And yet, if we as authors, take that chance and push our stories out into the world, then a wonderful thing happens. We suddenly have readers and I know, from experience, readers are amazing."

Daniel glanced over to the wings where Zeke and Ty were beaming at him. He could feel their love for him infuse his whole body, giving him the strength to continue. Turning back, he saw Pat give him the thumbs up and his smile widened.

"Our organizer, Graham Kirby, mentioned in his introduction that the internet has opened up a whole new world for authors and readers alike. No longer are authors strictly governed by a publisher's taste, or the current trend in reader preferences. We can write stories from the heart," Daniel tapped his chest with his free hand. "I write what feels real to me."

Daniel eyed the glass of water on the podium but decided not to risk it. He swallowed hard instead. "Within the romance genre, there are some people who dismiss the true mate trope, especially as it pertains to shifters as trite, unbelievable, or even, heaven's forbid, boring. I, clearly, don't believe that. I believe, in a world steeped with bad news, politics, wars, and the hatred that a few people have no problem expressing, that there will always be room for love and hope. That is what the romance genre is all about."

"Here, here," Stormy yelled, clapping wildly. In a split second everyone else was clapping, giving time for Daniel to gear himself up for the last part of the speech.

"I have a dream," he said when everyone had quietened down again, "and no, I am not giving *that* speech," a few laughs let him know the audience had got his reference, "but I hope with every story I put out, that if that story can make just one person smile. If that story can give five minutes relief to the reader from the realities they struggle with every day, whether it be illness, money worries, relationship issues, or so much more, I hope that for the short time they are reading, my readers are transported to a different world – an alternative reality if you will – where anything is possible. I hope, that for a short time, that reader is immersed in a world where love is the strongest force of all. Most of all, I hope, when that reader closes the final page, or flicks to the end of the story on their kindle, that they are left with a smile on their faces, and a warm glow in their heart. A glow they can hold close for a while as they go about their day."

One last bit, my sweet cub, you are doing brilliant. Daniel barely reacted as he heard Zeke's voice in his head, but he stood a little straighter, ready to deliver his conclusion. "Love comes in many forms and all of the wonderfully talented authors who are here today express that diversity in their characters and story lines. For me, true mates are not just a fictional concept. I have had more than one reader message me and let me know how they knew their partner was the one for them from the moment they met. I too, have been blessed recently with 'true mates' of my own." Daniel clumsily managed air quotes to show he was joking.

"But the thing to remember," he added as the audience chuckled, "is that among consenting adults there is no such thing as a love that's wrong. Love truly is a power available to all of us. It lives here, in our hearts," Daniel tapped his chest again, "and I believe that if there are days when it's difficult to remember that feeling, a good story reminds us of our dreams of how we'd like our world to be. In my world, that means complete with shifters, because I mean, wouldn't that be amazing? Wolves in the supermarket, hogging the meat section, or bears clustered around the honey aisle." The audience laughed just as Daniel had hoped.

"Finally, I just want to say, to all the authors who've brightened my life with their words, a huge thank you. And to my wonderful readers, words can't express what you all mean to me. Don't give up on love, because as my stories will show you time and time again, love hits you when you least expect it, and the Fates have a way of making things right. Thank you all for coming. Have a safe trip home."

As one, the audience rose to their feet, chanting his name, clapping so loud it was hurting Daniel's ears. But all Daniel could see was his mates, striding across the stage towards him, clapping as loudly as everyone else. Ducking back towards the microphone, Daniel said quickly, "And in case you're interested, these are my true mates in every sense of the word, Ty Hollifield and Zeke McIntyre everyone."

The crowd went crazy as Zeke grabbed him up and swung him around. Daniel's feet had barely hit the ground again, and Ty did the same thing. "You clever wee cub," Ty said fondly as he brushed a kiss against Daniel's ear. "You found a way to tell the truth after all."

Suddenly shaking, struck by the enormity of what he'd actually done,

Daniel could only nod and smile. *I hope one of you knows how to get me off this damn stage.*

Epilogue

Two weeks later

Zeke carefully stashed Daniel's laptop into his saddlebags and fixed the locks firmly. "That's it," he said, grinning at Ty who was already on his bike. "The house is locked up tight. The power is shut off. Daniel's precious laptop is secured, although, I doubt he's going to have any time to write where we're going."

"He's got a new idea for another book." Ty wagged his finger at his mate. "You know we promised him one hour every twenty four hours for writing. It was the only way we could get him to leave the house."

Zeke looked up at the log cabin with its wide windows and the hill beyond. "We've got somewhere to come back to now," he said softly. "A real home. Somehow, it makes going away all the more exciting."

"I know what you mean. The Fates definitely know what they're doing.

Just imagine, how awkward things could've been if our sweet cub had been a traveler too? We could've roamed this country for another ten years before we found him."

"Or we may have found him sooner. There's no way of knowing and personally I don't care. We've found him now and that's the important thing." Zeke shrugged, swinging his leg over his bike. "But, ten points for suggesting our sweet cub let his bear out while we got the packing finished. Hopefully he'll be a lot more relaxed about our trip this time."

"Will you be?" Ty kicked his bike over, "We know a lot of those bikers we're running with this time don't have a problem spending time with a sweet young morsel like our mate."

"Why do you think I've been chopping so much wood?" Zeke yelled as flexed his biceps. "Ain't no one going to get near our sweet cub." The sound of his bike's engine filled the air, the throb of the bike a familiar friend between his legs. Peeling down the driveway, Zeke and Ty rode the four miles to the parking spot in the forest where they'd dropped Daniel off an hour before. Zeke felt his phone vibrate in his pocket as he parked. Stopping the engine, he pulled out his phone. "It's Morty," he said to Ty. "You go find our cub, I'll just answer this."

"Tell Morty hello from me." Grabbing Daniel's clothes from his backpack, Ty sauntered across the grass, heading for the trees.

Zeke accepted the call. "Hi, Bro, how goes the feeling following?"

"He's leading me a merry chase," Morty said wryly. "It seems the fates saw fit to bless me with a sweet omega pup."

"Pup not cub?" Zeke laughed.

"A wolf pup whose part of a pack that don't want to let him go."

"You knew there was always a possibility you might have to adapt your life to your mate. Why can't you stay with him?"

"His alpha won't let a bear in the pack," Morty sighed. "I don't know what the fuck to do. This is tearing us apart. I haven't seen him in three days and I'm worried sick about him. That alpha of his is a real piece of work."

Zeke thought quickly. "Where are you?"

"Albuquerque. I followed him there after we met in Roswell."

"It'll take us two days to get there, but we're already packed. We're just picking up Daniel now. He's having a run."

"I'm not sure the alpha will be thrilled to see another three bears in town," Morty warned. "I'm under strict orders not to go within a mile of pack territory. I'd fucking ignore the lot of them and go in there anyway, but there is a lot of them and I don't want them to hurt my sweet mate to get at me."

"We'll be there as quick as we can to back you up. A trip is a trip, bro, and besides, if you decide to do a spot of kidnapping, you'll need an alibi and back up.

"Don't think I haven't thought of kidnapping him, but it's complicated," Morty growled. "Thanks, you know, just thanks."

"You can tell us about it when we get there. Book us a room and for fuck's sake, make sure it has a custom king bed or Daniel will have a fit. Later, bro."

Closing down the screen, Zeke tucked his phone back in his pocket, his mind already making changes to their itinerary. He and Ty came across a lot of wolves in their traveling days, but they made a point of steering clear of pack territory. Solitary, or lone wolves as they were called never seemed to have a problem with other shifter types. Packs, however, were a different story. Pack wolves were as territorial as hell, and the fact Morty's mate was an omega wolf could be a real concern as many packs considered them the bottom of their precious hierarchy. "I'm not letting some bloody pack alpha keep my brother from claiming his mate," he muttered as he strode through the tree line. Spotting Ty hiding behind a large tree, his frown deepened as he joined his mate as silently as possible.

"What's going on?" Zeke whispered.

"It's our cub," Ty chuckled. "Look over there. Remember the first time we saw him?"

Following Ty's finger, Zeke's eyes widened as he saw what Ty was so amused about. Their gorgeous cub was rolling around in the grass, the golden highlights in his fur glinting in the sun. But it wasn't the fact Daniel was having so much fun in his bear form that made Zeke smile. It was the blue stains around his muzzle and front paws. Their cub must have found some late blooming blueberries.

"Do we have time to play with him in our bear form?" Ty asked, already pulling off his shirt. "He's having so much fun."

"We're going to have to give the toy run a miss anyway," Zeke said, following his mate's lead and tugging at his clothing. "Morty needs help with a wolf pack in Albuquerque. I told him we'd be there in two days."

"And we will," Ty shoved his jeans down his legs and toed off his boots. "That's what family does. But we've got time for this, surely. Just half an hour."

Ty was right, and Zeke's bear was as keen to play with their cub as Zeke was. Shedding the last of his clothes, Zeke encouraged his bear spirit to take over, his body expanding as his jaw changed, and fur appeared.

Chuffing at Ty who'd also shifted, Zeke ambled out of the trees, able to sense the moment Daniel knew they were there. The cub paused mid-roll and then floundered as his body weight tipped him over to one side.

Oops. I found blueberries, Daniel's voice sounded breathless in Zeke's head. *Do you want to see? There's plenty left, I didn't eat them all.*

Sure, little cub show us where they are, Zeke sent back and as Daniel rolled himself onto his feet and ambled away, Zeke couldn't help adding, *I'd follow that ass anywhere.*

My furry ass? Really? Daniel peered over his shoulder at him.

Furry or smooth, Ty's voice chimed in. *Babe, we will follow you to the ends of the earth and back.*

I'm only going over the hill a ways. But there was a spring in Daniel's step as he led them to where he'd found more berry bushes.

This is home, my mate, Ty targeted Zeke this time. *A real home, all thanks to our cub.*

A cub who's good at finding blueberries, Zeke agreed. He was really glad for his black fur. It really wouldn't do for a bear of his age and size to be running around with blueberry stains on his paws. Yes, they needed to get on the road soon, and there was the issue with Morty to help out with. But for a bear, warm sun and blueberries was a wonderful way to spend a bit of time, especially when accompanied by his loving mates.

The End

As you can guess, there will likely be a sequel to this book. It wasn't intentional, but Morty came through so clearly to me, I really felt he deserved his mate.

Thank you so much for reading this far. Those of you who follow me on social media know that I suffered badly from burn out over the past few months, and this is the first book I've been able to write since coming out from a depressive slump. I may not be a bear shifter, but the feelings Daniel expressed, both in his anxiety in meeting new people and facing new situations, and the speech he gave at the conference all came from my heart. I can only hope my indulgence, in sharing some of my personal feelings through this story has still meant it was an enjoyable one for you.

With the New Year fast approaching, my "to write" list is getting longer, but I am facing it with a new and improved enthusiasm thanks in part to the huge support I've had from my readers during my difficult times. The final Necromancer story is waiting to be written, I have books planned in the Gods series, Arrowtown, Balance, Northern States Pack, the City Dragon's series and of course, the final book in the Cloverleah Pack series to finish. I owe you all a huge vote of thanks for being patient with me with this story, as I know it wasn't one any of you expected.

As always, if this story did leave you with a smile on your face, please leave me a short review at your place of purchase. Reviews are a lifeblood for any author, and extremely helpful in securing new readers. With piracy on the rise, and the clamp downs by social media platforms on any MM promotion, authors need all the help they can get.

Finally, from me, Zeus and Hades (who have been snoring in my earhole for much of the writing of this story), I'd like to wish you all the love and laughter you deserve in the coming year.

Hug the one you love,

Lisa xx

About the Author

Lisa Oliver had been writing non-fiction books for years when visions of half dressed, buff men started invading her dreams. Unable to resist the lure of her stories, Lisa decided to switch to fiction books, and now stories about her men clamor to get out from under her fingertips. With over fifty MM true mate titles to her credit so far, Lisa shows no sign of slowing down.

When Lisa is not writing, she is usually reading with a cup of tea always at hand. Her grown children and grandchildren sometimes try and pry her away from the computer and have found that the best way to do it is to promise her chocolate. Lisa will do anything for chocolate.

Lisa loves to hear from her readers and other writers (I really do, lol). You can catch up with her on any of the social media links below.

Facebook – http://www.facebook.com/lisaoliverauthor

Official Author page – https://www.facebook.com/LisaOliverManloveAuthor/

My new private teaser group - https://www.facebook.com/groups/540361549650663/

And I am now on MeWe – you can find my group at http://mewe.com/join/lisa_olivers_paranormal_pack

My blog - (http://www.supernaturalsmut.com)

Twitter – http://www.twitter.com/wisecrone333

Email me directly at yoursintuitively@gmail.com.

Other Books By Lisa/Lee Oliver

Please note, I have now marked the books that contain mpreg and MMM for those of you who don't like to read those type of stories. Hope that helps ☺

Cloverleah Pack

Book 1 – The Reluctant Wolf – Kane and Shawn

Book 2 – The Runaway Cat – Griff and Diablo

Book 3 – When No Doesn't Cut It – Damien and Scott

Book 3.5 – Never Go Back – Scott and Damien's Trip and a free story about Malacai and Elijah

Book 4 – Calming the Enforcer – Troy and Anton

Book 5 – Getting Close to the Omega – Dean and Matthew

Book 6 – Fae for All – Jax, Aelfric and Fafnir (M/M/M)

Book 7 – Watching Out for Fangs – Josh and Vadim

Book 8 – Tangling with Bears – Tobias, Luke and Kurt (M/M/M)

Book 9 – Angel in Black Leather – Adair and Vassago

Book 9.5 – Scenes from Cloverleah – four short stories featuring the men we've come to love

Book 10 – On The Brink – Teilo, Raff and Nereus (M/M/M)

Book 11 – Don't Tempt Fate – Marius and Cathair

Book 12 – My Treasure to Keep – Thomas and Ivan

Book 13 – is on the list to be written – it will be about Wesley and yes, he will find his mate too, but that's all I can say about this one for now ☺ (Coming soon)

The Gods Made Me Do It
(Cloverleah spin off series)

Book One - Get Over It – Madison and Sebastian's story

Book Two - You've Got to be Kidding – Poseidon and Claude (mpreg)

Book Three – Don't Fight It – Lasse and Jason

Book Four – Riding the Storm – Thor and Orin (mpreg elements [Jason from previous book gives birth in this one])

The Necromancer's Smile (This is a trilogy series under the name The Necromancer's Smile where the main couple, Dakar and Sy are the focus of all three books – these cannot be read as standalone).

Book One – Dakar and Sy – The Meeting

Book Two – Dakar and Sy – Family affairs

Book Three – Dakar and Sy – Taking Care of Business – (coming soon).

Bound and Bonded Series

Book One – Don't Touch – Levi and Steel

Book Two – Topping the Dom – Pearson and Dante

Book Three – Total Submission – Kyle and Teric

Book Four – Fighting Fangs – Ace and Devin

Book Five – No Mate of Mine – Roger and Cam

Book Six – Undesirable Mate – Phillip and Kellen

Stockton Wolves Series

Book One – Get off My Case – Shane and Dimitri

Book Two – Copping a Lot of Sin – Ben, Sin and Gabriel (M/M/M)

Book Three – Mace's Awakening – Mace and Roan

Book Four – Don't Bite – Trent and Alexi

Book Five – Tell Me the Truth – Captain Reynolds and Nico (mpreg)

Alpha and Omega Series

Book One – The Biker's Omega – Marly and Trent

Book Two – Dance Around the Cop – Zander and Terry

Book 2.5 – Change of Plans - Q and Sully

Book Three – The Artist and His Alpha – Caden and Sean

Book Four – Harder in Heels – Ronan and Asaph

Book 4.5 – A Touch of Spring – Bronson and Harley

Book Five – If You Can't Stand The Heat – Wyatt and Stone (Previously published in an anthology)

Book Six – Fagin's Folly – Fagin and Cooper

Book Seven – The Cub and His Alphas – Daniel, Zeke and Ty (MMM)

Spin off from The Biker's Omega – BBQ, Bikes, and Bears – Clive and Roy

There will be more A&O books – I have had one teasing my brain for months, so stay tuned for that one.

Balance – Angels and Demons

The Viper's Heart – Raziel and Botis

Passion Punched King – Anael and Zagan

(Uriel and Haures's story will be coming soon)

Arrowtown

A Tiger's Tale – Ra and Seth (mpreg)

Snake Snack – Simon and Darwin (mpreg)

Liam's Lament – Liam Beau and Trent (MMM) (Mpreg)

Doc's Deputy – Deputy Joe and Doc (Mpreg)

NEW Series – City Dragons

Dragon's Heat – Dirk and Jon

Dragon's Fire – Samuel and Raoul

Dragon's Tears – (coming soon)

Standalone:

Bound by Blood – Max and Lyle – (a spin off from Cloverleah Pack #7)

The Power of the Bite – Dax and Zane

One Wrong Step – Robert and Syron

Uncaged – Carlin and Lucas (Shifter's Uprising in conjunction with Thomas Oliver)

Also under the penname Lee Oliver

Northern States Pack Series

Book One – Ranger's End Game – Ranger and Aiden

Book Two – Cam's Promise – Cam and Levi

Book Three – Under Sean's Protection – Sean and Kyle – (Coming soon)

Printed in Poland
by Amazon Fulfillment
Poland Sp. z o.o., Wrocław

54684729R00184